About the Author

It was as a teacher and parent that Rose Impey first started telling her own stories, and they were so well received she soon started writing them down. Rose has fantastic credentials with young readers – in particular as the creator of the best-selling *Sleepover Club* books. Rose lives in Leicestershire where she does not have a scary fairy godmother, but she does have some very funky boots!

For Bren and her kids
and for Pascale who rode the ride for me
R.I.

ORCHARD BOOKS
96 Leonard Street, London EC2A 4XD
Orchard Books Australia
32/45-51 Huntley Street, Alexandria, NSW 2015
ISBN 1 84362 683 7
First published in Great Britain in 2005
A paperback original
Text © Rose Impey 2005
The right of Rose Impey to be identified as the author of this
work has been asserted by her in accordance with
the Copyright, Designs and Patents Act, 1988.
A CIP catalogue record for this book is available
from the British Library.
5 7 9 10 8 6 4
Printed in Great Britain

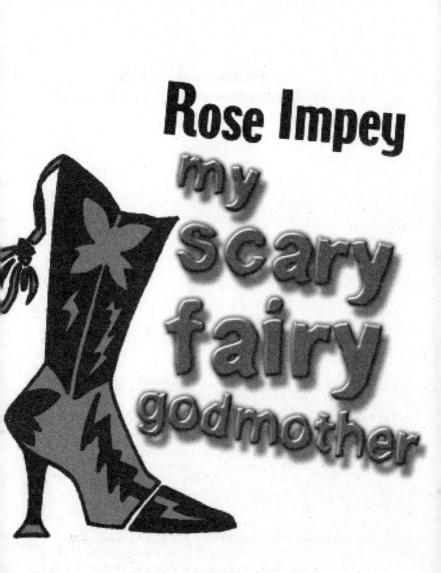

Rose Impey

my scary fairy godmother

ORCHARD BOOKS

one

Everyone should have a fairy godmother – right? But until I went to stay with my cousin, Maxine, I used to think they only existed in fairy stories. But Max turned out to be one scary fairy godmother and she changed my life. For ever.

Before that, I was boring little Bella – quiet and shy, with mousy hair and terrible clothes. Not any more, though. You're talking to the new, improved model. I've even got a new name: Izzy. How cool is that?

Now I'm going to tell you how she did it – the whole story, like Max would say: with all the grisly details.

It started the day I went to stay in Manchester with the Rosses. I really didn't want to go; I hardly knew them. My mum and Auntie Paula are sisters, but they rarely spoke now they were grown up, so I hadn't seen any of the family since I was little. But when Mum got ill, and had to go into hospital, there was nowhere else for me to go.

The afternoon Uncle Dougie was coming to

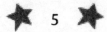

collect me, I remember standing there, all pathetic, with my case packed, like one of those evacuee kids in the war. I felt so scared I could hardly bear to look at my mum.

'Come on, Isabella, cheer up,' Mum said, her arm round my shoulder, trying her best to smile. 'It's only for a week or two. I'll ring or write to you every day. And it's not that far.'

Not that far?! It was *two hundred miles!* She might as well have been sending me to live on Mars as far as I was concerned. And when I arrived there, it couldn't have felt much weirder if she had.

Everything was different from home. It's a city for a start, nothing like the little town where I live. And their house is much bigger than ours, with this huge kitchen that everyone seems to collect in. They were all waiting there when I arrived, the whole lot of them, like a reception committee. Auntie Paula came over and gave me a big hug. Even though she's older than Mum she looks younger, trendier, with short hair and her ears pierced in two or three places. She's very smiley and seemed nice, but I could have done without all the hugging!

'Come and sit down, Isabella, luv,' she said. 'How was the journey?'

'OK,' I shrugged, which wasn't the truth, it had felt really awkward.

'I've no ears left,' Uncle Dougie said, 'she's about talked them off,' which I think was supposed to be a joke because I hadn't actually said a word for most of the journey. I wasn't used to talking to almost strangers.

My cousin Maxine and her best friend, Leah, were there – giving me the once over and grinning at each other. I was sure they were laughing at me and I wanted the floor to open up and swallow me. Max and Leah are fifteen and really cool-looking. Just like pop stars – the hair, the clothes, everything. Next to them, I felt like a little shadow.

'Hi, hon,' Max said, grinning, 'welcome to the House of Fun.'

'Guaranteed laugh-a-minute,' Leah said, rolling her eyes and the two of them high-fived.

Even my cousin Martin was there, which Max said was a miracle.

'Mum must've bribed him,' she told me. 'It's the only way she'd have got him away from his computer.'

At least Martin didn't stare at me. When Auntie Paula asked him wasn't he at least going to say hello, he just ducked his head and grunted. I didn't say anything, either. I wasn't used to talking to boys.

When it was time for supper, which is what the Rosses call it, that was different too. Mum and me

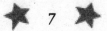

call it tea and we just have something on our knees, watching the telly. Mum isn't really into cooking. But Auntie Paula makes these big casseroles and everyone sits round a table, talking at the tops of their voices. I wasn't hungry; I was far too nervous to eat, so I just poked at it with a fork and *pretended* to eat. Everyone was making jokes. Mostly about how much Martin eats. Nobody calls him Martin, by the way, they usually call him Chip, but at meal-times they call him *The Hoover.*

'Look out, The Hoover's about. Eat up Isabella.'

'Leave the pattern on the plate,' they told him.

Martin took no notice. He just kept sucking up food like a…hoover. Before we'd finished eating, his best friend turned up at the door. Max told me that, because his name's Danny *Pike*, everyone at school calls them Fish and Chips.

Danny came and sat at the table with us, but didn't join in because apparently he doesn't eat much. Not like Chip. Uncle Dougie said, he eats like Desperate Dan on his birthday.

'Another helping of Cow Pie for The Hoover?'

Max and Leah watched Chip tuck into his fourth helping and groaned.

'Why are brothers so disgusting?' said Max.

'It's an extra gene,' said Leah, who had two brothers of her own. 'The *disgusting* gene.'

'Yeah,' said Max, 'Chip's got a bundle of them,'

and they both fell about laughing, even Auntie Paula joined in.

Usually my mum and me eat our tea watching *Neighbours*. We don't *talk* all the time like the Rosses. That first mealtime with them felt a bit like a game of netball, which is another thing I've never been any good at. You know, not being sure when the ball's coming your way but knowing when it does, you're bound to drop it. When they weren't teasing Chip, everyone was firing questions at me – about school, and friends, and what I was interested in, and what I liked to eat – that kind of stuff. I didn't tell them much; there wasn't much to tell. But they still kept asking.

I couldn't wait for the meal to be over so I could go and just sit on my bed and be on my own. At home I spend a lot of time in my bedroom. I've never had to share it with anyone else – *ever*. So imagine how I felt when Auntie Paula told Max to take my case up to her bedroom and Max said, 'C'mon, hon. Let's go. You're bunking with me. Won't that be fun!'

two

Max and Leah sat on Max's bed and I sat opposite them on the spare bed. They kept talking about music and clothes and boys and other things I didn't know a whole lot about. I knew they were trying to be nice, trying to get to know me, but the harder they tried the more nervous and embarrassed I got. When the phone rang downstairs and Auntie Paula called up that it was Mum ringing for me, I felt like I'd been rescued from the torture chamber.

Auntie Paula was in the kitchen, listening to the radio while she did the washing up. When she handed me the phone – it was one of those walkabout ones – I didn't know where to go so as not to be in anybody's way. It was too noisy in the kitchen so I tried the lounge, but Uncle Dougie was asleep in front of the TV. In the end, I went and sat on the stairs.

'Hello, sweetie,' Mum said. 'Everything OK? I'm missing you already.'

I had to swallow really hard. I wanted to tell her how much I was missing her too. I wanted to beg

her to let me come home, but I was scared that if I opened my mouth properly I'd start bawling, and someone might hear me. So I just mumbled, 'Mmm,' to everything Mum asked me. I didn't take a lot of it in.

'Anyway, I'll ring you again tomorrow,' she said finally, 'and on Monday I'll let you know how I get on at the hospital. But don't worry, now, I'm going to be just fine. You'll be back home in no time. You will be a good girl for your Auntie Paula, won't you?'

'Mmm. Bye, Mum,' I said. After she'd hung up, I sat there on the stairs, squeezing the phone hard, trying not to cry. I was worried for myself, having to stay in Manchester, with people I hardly knew, but I was worried for my mum too, having to go into hospital, all on her own. I knew she was trying to be brave, but that meant I had to be too, even though I definitely wasn't feeling it.

While I was still sitting there, I heard voices coming from Max's room. I wasn't trying to eavesdrop, honest. But once I'd started, I was stuck. If I'd got up and moved, Max and Leah might have heard me. You know what happens to people who listen into other people's conversations, though – sometimes they hear things they'd rather not.

'So what're you gonna do with her, Max?' Leah was asking. 'They're gonna eat her alive at school.'

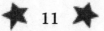 11

'Tell me something I don't know, Leah.'

'That straggly hair and those clothes!'

'I'm never gonna live it down,' Max groaned. 'And she's such a mouse. She's hardly said two words to us yet.'

'You know what *she* needs, don't you?' said Leah.

'Yeah,' said Max. '*The Full Works.*'

'But d'you think she'll go for it?'

'Leave her to me,' said Max. 'I'll make an excellent fairy godmother. And when I've worked my magic, this Cinderella's gonna be the talk of the school.'

I sat there on the stairs like a little rabbit. I couldn't begin to guess what Max was planning. I didn't know what The Full Works was, but whatever it was, it sounded like the start of something big. And it certainly was!

I don't know about you, but I've never been good at waking up in the morning. On school days my mum's usually in and out like a yoyo – chivvy, chivvy, chivvy – until I get out of bed. So that first morning away from home it took me ages to wake up properly. At first I couldn't work out where I was, but I had this creepy feeling that someone was watching me. When I opened my eyes – someone was.

Max was sitting up in bed, staring at me. She'd

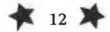

got a sketchpad leaning against her knees and she was sucking on the end of a pencil. Her bed was littered with magazines.

'I thought you were never gonna wake up,' she said. 'Come on, we've got a busy day. What d'you think of these?'

Three or four magazines winged their way across the room and landed on my bed. I sat up and started to leaf through them. Max had turned down the corners on some pages, so I studied those more carefully. But I still had no idea what I was supposed to be looking at. Max soon got fed up of my blank looks. She jumped out of her bed and came and sat on the end of mine.

'We're looking for a whole new image,' she explained. 'Nothing regular – like townie or skater. And too glam won't work – you're definitely not a girlie-girl. I'm thinking more indie. Perhaps a bit retro on the surface, but underneath...this *wild child* trying to get out. What d'you think?'

I was starting to think perhaps I hadn't woken up yet, that this was still part of my dream. What was Max talking about? But slowly I began to realise. She was planning to *make me over*. That's what all the talk about Cinderella and fairy godmothers had been about.

'I'm a bit of a Makeover Queen, if I say so myself,' Max said. 'I love those programmes, don't you? I did a *Changing Rooms* in here last summer. Random, right?'

I looked around Max's room, which *is* fantastic. The walls are a groovy turquoise blue, so it feels like you're underwater, and there's lots of gold and silver everywhere. One wall's covered with posters and photos and bits of Max's art projects. It certainly is random. And wonderful, but even so...

'Relax, hon! You've either got good taste, or you haven't,' Max rattled on. 'And as you can see – I've got it.'

Max was right: everything about her was *really* cool. But I didn't feel relaxed – terrified, more like. Max was too excited to notice, though.

'No need to thank me, either,' she went on. 'We're family, right. And let's face it, my cool-cred would hit the floor if I let you go out looking like that. So, think of it as self-preservation.'

All the time Max was talking she was drawing in her pad, and checking out colours. 'Pink,' she eventually decided. 'Definitely pink. Not baby pink! Hot, fruity, juicy pink. I'm thinking raspberries. With black. Great combination. Well-sexy.'

I sat in bed, not really believing what was happening. Just the *word* 'sexy' made me go red. I was used to disappearing into the background and that's what I wanted to go on doing. But I wouldn't have dared to argue with Max, that would have felt like standing in front of a steamroller. I'm telling you, she was scary!

Eventually, she paused for breath and gave me a quick smile.

'OK, we'll work the rest out as we go along,' she said. 'But prepare to be amazed. When I'm finished, I guarantee even your own mum won't recognise you. You've got ten minutes to get some breakfast. Chop, chop, Cinderella. We've got a makeover to do.'

three

In no more than ten minutes I was sitting on a chair in Max's bedroom with a towel round my shoulders, waiting for what Maxine called Phase One of the makeover to start! I dreaded to think how many other phases she'd got planned! It was Saturday morning, so Auntie Paula and Uncle Dougie had gone to the supermarket; we had the house to ourselves. Chip wouldn't bother us, Max said, he'd be in one of his two usual states, fast asleep or super-glued to his computer.

Max had an apron on, with combs and brushes sticking out of the pockets. And a scarily sharp looking pair of scissors in her hand. By now Leah had arrived and was sitting on Max's bed, breaking up metal coat hangers and giving advice. Leah's sister is a hairdresser, which was where the scissors had come from.

Max had sat me in front of a full-length mirror, but before she got started she covered the glass with a long scarf, so I couldn't see what was happening. I didn't know if that was a good thing or not. There were suddenly loads of questions I

wanted to ask Max like: had she ever cut anybody's hair before? How much hair was she planning on leaving me with? What would my mum have to say about it? What on earth were the broken coat hangers for? As usual, I was far too much of a coward to say any of them out loud.

But, although I was feeling petrified, there was this teeny-tiny voice inside me asking another question: could Max *really, honestly, truly* turn me into someone else? Someone more interesting? Someone even I wouldn't recognise? Because, although it was scary, that was sort of exciting as well. I've always wished I wasn't so quiet – and boring. I've often wondered what it would be like to be prettier, more popular, cool even. Maybe that's the reason why, although I'd been growing my hair since I was a toddler, I didn't try to stop Max. I just closed my eyes and left it all to my new, scary fairy godmother.

If I'm really honest, it didn't feel like I had a whole lot of choice anyway.

Max and Leah were arguing about *feathering* and *layering* and whether perms were out of fashion or coming back in. And about something called *Zig-Zagging*. Then, suddenly, I heard the scissors *snip, snap*, round my ears and Max's surprised voice, 'Oo-err. Well, we've started now…'

I tried to stay calm, but after a bit I couldn't help taking a peep. When I saw the amount of

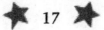

hair on the floor, I panicked and jumped out of the chair.

'I must be nearly bald!' I screamed.

Max went mad. 'Look out, idiot! I almost chopped your ear off. What's up, don't you trust me? Go on then, have a feel. See, there's still plenty left.'

Actually, there was. It was a bit shorter in places but I could still feel plenty around my shoulders. I sat back in the chair and tried to relax. And I was doing OK, until Max asked Leah if she'd brought the colours, and Leah said she'd brought *Raspberry Ripple* and *Crimson Craze* so which did she want, and Max said, 'Let's go mad. Why don't we have both?'

I tried to make a run for it then. I was imagining my head looking like a striped ice cream. But Max grabbed me and held me back in the chair.

'Calm down, girl. We're only doing the odd stripe of each. It'll be very subtle. Remember, I'm your fairy godmother; you can trust me. Now come on everyone – bathroom.'

Max locked the three of us in the bathroom for what seemed like ages. Chip was awake by then, knocking on the door and rattling the handle to get in. 'What're you lot up to, anyway?' he eventually shouted. 'You've been in there half an hour already.'

'Girls' stuff,' Max told him. 'Come back in

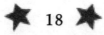

fifteen minutes.'

'Fifteen minutes! I can't wait that long.'

"Course you can,' Max called back.

'He can tie a knot in it,' Leah grinned and they fell about laughing again.

They'd covered strips of my hair with this gooey stuff and then wrapped it in bits of foil. The three of us were perched on the side of the bath, waiting for the colour to take. I watched Max and Leah doing their nails and listened to them talking about people from school. I was trying to imagine what I was going to look like with *pink* hair and dreading to think what my mum was going to say.

At last, Leah checked Max's watch and said it was time to wash it off.

As I leaned over the washbasin, I could see that the water going down the sink was the colour of Ribena.

So I was already feeling nervous without Chip stirring things up. When we came out of the bathroom he was waiting outside, leaning against the wall with his legs crossed. When he saw me, his mouth opened and closed like a goldfish.

'Oh – my – G-d! What on earth happened to her? Mum is gonna flip!'

Max told him to zip it and bundled me back into the bedroom. She still wouldn't let me see it. She towelled my hair dry and then, while Max

 19

started winding pieces of hair round the bits of coat hanger, Leah went downstairs to find a new roll of kitchen foil.

When she came back, Leah whispered to Max that her mum and dad were home. Max swore under her breath and quickly locked her bedroom door which had me panicking all over again. By then I was actually glad they'd covered the mirror. I was glad I couldn't see what was going on.

Between them Max and Leah covered the hair that was wrapped round bits of coat hanger with more foil and then heated them all up with Max's hair straighteners. It was a pity they hadn't put a peg on my nose as well, because then I wouldn't have smelled the burning smell which I suddenly realised must be my hair. Max and Leah started blaming each other.

'Too hot, too hot. You've got them too hot!'

'Yes! I think I know that, Leah! Timing was your job.'

'You're the one with the watch...'

'Well, I can't do everything!'

Eventually, it was finished. They took all the stuff off my hair and both of them kept circling round me, fluffing it up and fiddling with it.

'Oh, yes, this is *sweet*,' Max decided. 'If I say so myself: I'm a genius.'

'Give me some of the credit, why don't

you?' Leah complained.

I thought they'd let me see it then, but Max said, 'Just needs a bit of make-up,' and Leah agreed.

I tried to argue with them but they promised me they just meant a touch of lip gloss. 'And some pink glitter,' Leah added quickly. I was so glad my mum wasn't going to see it.

They finally agreed it was time to show me the results of all their hard work. But just as Max was about to take the scarf off the mirror, Auntie Paula banged on the bedroom door, demanding to come in.

'Exactly what's going on in there, Maxine?' she shouted. 'And, more to the point, what's that burning smell?'

One quick look round and I knew we were in big trouble. The room was in chaos: hair all over the floor, and broken bits of coat hangers and screwed up foil. So much pinky-red dye on the towels it looked like someone had been murdered. *And* it smelled like we'd been having a bonfire.

But Auntie Paula wasn't going away, so Max had no choice but to unlock the door. Her mum stormed in like a tornado. I thought my mum had a temper but Auntie Paula's yelling sort of bounced off the ceiling.

Even so, I hardly took in a word of what she was saying...because in all the chaos, the scarf

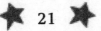

covering the mirror had fallen away and there, looking back at me, was this weird-looking person, with a mixture of straight and kinky, pink and brown hair, shiny lips and pink glittery eyes. *Scary!*

Suddenly I realised who it was.

Well, I thought, Max was right about one thing – even my own mum wouldn't recognise me. And I slid off the chair onto the floor and burst out crying.

four

'What *on earth* were you thinking?!' Auntie Paula asked Max for the fifth time. We were all sitting round the kitchen table while Auntie Paula tried to get to the bottom of what was going on.

'Look, Mum,' said Max, perfectly calmly, '*something* had to happen. Otherwise they'd have made mincemeat of her at school on Monday.'

'But Isabella may only be at your school for two weeks!'

'Two hours'd be enough,' Max told her, 'if you look that different. Even you've got to admit it, Mum – it's an improvement.'

Auntie Paula wasn't admitting anything and anyway, she said, 'Look how upset Isabella is.'

'We should've prepared her better, Max,' Leah admitted, handing me more tissues.

'Thanks, Leah. Tell me something I don't know,' Max snapped back.

But I wasn't crying because they hadn't prepared me, or because I didn't like my new hairstyle. To be honest it looked...*amazing!* The problem was, it looked rubbish on *me*. You've seen those books with split pages, where you put different heads on people's bodies so they look *really* silly. Well, imagine that times ten. I'm sitting there, dressed in my pyjamas, with this really groovy hairstyle and funky make-up, but underneath it's still mousy-me, with red eyes and a runny nose.

It didn't take long for Max and Leah to work that out, though.

'It's bound to look a bit strange,' Leah said, 'with only the hair done.'

'Yeah,' Max agreed, 'you've got to imagine how you'll look – and feel – when you've had The Full Works.' She kept on saying that, but I still had no idea what it meant exactly.

Auntie Paula could obviously see where it was all leading, though. 'Stop right there!' she said. 'We're having no more transformations, thank you very much. You've done quite enough already. And that, Maxine, is my last word.'

Except that Max managed to have the *last* last word, as I was beginning to discover she usually did.

She'd already explained to me that her school, Rowan Park High, didn't exactly have a uniform. They have something called a dress code, which means they can pretty well please themselves, as long as it's not too extreme.

Now Max smiled sweetly at Auntie Paula, 'OK.

Whatever you say, Mum. You're the boss. But you've seen Isabella's school clothes, right? You won't mind if she's completely destroyed on Monday? You don't mind having that on your conscience?'

'Oh, Max, for goodness sake, stop dramatising,' said Auntie Paula. 'And stop frightening Isabella.'

'The thing is, Mum,' said Max, 'you probably won't understand that her school uniform looks like something out of the Dark Ages because that's roughly when you and Dad were at school.'

Uncle Dougie grunted and told Max to leave him out of it. He'd been keeping his head down, reading the newspaper with his sunglasses on because he said my hair was so bright it was giving him a headache.

Chip had been drawn downstairs by the shouting. He surprised everyone, especially Max, by suddenly offering his opinion. 'I don't think it's that bad,' he said. 'Least it won't be – when you've evened it up.'

'It's not meant to be *even*, dummy,' Max snarled at him. 'And since when were you a style consultant?'

Auntie Paula sighed, 'Perhaps Chip's right. Leah's sister could even it up.'

'It's meant to be *random!*' Max and Leah shouted together.

Auntie Paula just kept shaking her head, 'I

don't know. I really don't. And what on earth am I going to tell Isabella's mum?'

That was worrying me too. I thought my mum would never get over the shock. I was quite relieved when Chip changed the subject by asking if we were ever getting any lunch today? Auntie Paula took a break from telling us off to make bacon sandwiches for everyone, apart from Leah who had to go home to babysit her kid brothers.

We ate lunch almost in silence, which wasn't as much of a relief as I'd thought it would be. I was glad when it was over, but when the others disappeared, I hung around for a while to help Auntie Paula clear up and load the dishwasher. She seemed surprised – I don't think Max and Chip ever helped unless they were chivvied, but I always do that stuff at home for Mum.

When I followed Max up to her bedroom I was feeling bad that I'd got her into trouble with her mum, when she'd only been trying to help me. I thought she might be cross with me, but she didn't seem the least bit bothered.

'Oh, don't worry about Mum,' Max told me lightly. 'She'll get over it. She always does. She's like the weather – blows up a storm and then the clouds pass and the sun comes out.'

Then Max threw open her wardrobe doors. 'Anyway, babe. Ready for Phase Two?'

Phase Two?! I'd barely recovered from Phase One. Why couldn't Max see it was never going to work, anyway? If anything I looked worse than before. Sillier!

But Max was already busy, riffling through her wardrobe, pulling out clothes of her own to dress me up in. I felt really self-conscious, standing there in my underwear, while she dragged things over my head or told me to step into things: hipster jeans that fell to my knees if I didn't hold them up, V-neck sweaters that plunged to my waist, mini-skirts that would have wrapped round me twice. Max is much bigger than me and everything of hers totally drowned me. I looked ridiculous in everything. Finally, even she had to admit defeat.

She opened her desk drawer and got out her latest bank statement.

'Twenty-five measly quid!' she said, looking disappointed. 'That won't go far, still it's a start. Come on, girl. Let's go get you some new clothes.'

I couldn't believe it. Max was prepared to spend her own money on me! So, even though I had a feeling that a shopping trip with Max might be another disaster-area, I suddenly found myself telling her that she didn't need to use her own money. I'd got some money of my own – two hundred pounds in my savings account.

'Two hundred quid!' Max whistled. 'Hello, Miss

Moneybags! Where did you get all that?'

I told her I'd been saving for ages. But when she asked me what for, I had no idea.

'My mum thinks saving's a good habit to get into,' I told Max. 'She always says you never know when you might need something for a rainy day.'

'Well, it's raining cats and dogs today,' Max grinned at me. 'Come on, Cinderella, your fairy godmother's gonna get you ready for the ball.'

five

Going shopping with Max wasn't like any shopping I'd ever done before. I'd never been without my mum for a start. Most Saturdays, before she got ill, we used to take the bus into town. But it's only a little town, nothing like Manchester. We'd look in the same few clothes shops every week, but we wouldn't often try anything on. And we'd hardly ever buy anything. Mum usually said the clothes weren't worth the money and she could easily have made them for half the price if she only had the time. But she never had. And, since she'd been ill, she'd been too tired even to window shop.

It was completely different with Max. She knew all the cool places to go and where to get real bargains. Max tried on one or two things, but she spent most of her time bringing armfuls of clothes to the changing room for me to try on. Things I'd never have chosen for myself in a million years. Way-out, wild things.

There was a tiny, little black denim skirt that I tried to tell Max I couldn't wear because it barely

covered my bottom. Max just shook her head in despair at me and came back with these wild rainbow tights to wear with it. And a sweater in the magic pink and black colours.

'That outfit really rocks.' Max insisted, 'You're getting it. No discussion.'

Max was so scary, I didn't dare argue with her. And she was really embarrassing too when she said things like, 'OK, babe, you'd better be Trinnie 'cos you've got no tits, and I'll be Susannah.'

Max couldn't believe I didn't know who they were. 'Off *What Not to Wear*?' she said, like I must be an alien or something.

She told me they were these two fashion experts who turned people from desperate no-hopers into quite normal human beings. So there was hope for me yet, she said. 'Just joking.'

As we were going round, Max gave me a few fashion tips too. 'Never be a fashion slave, Izzy,' she warned me. 'Don't try to look like anyone else. You've gotta be your own person. You've gotta stand out from the crowd, if you wanna get noticed, get people talking.'

To begin with, every time I spotted my hair in a changing-room mirror, it gave me a real shock, but by the end of the afternoon I was starting to get a little more used to it. In fact, in some of the outfits that Max had chosen for me, it looked

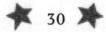

good and I could sort of see what Max was trying to turn me into. Once or twice I even thought: wow, is that really me? Because I looked so different and...I don't know...*almost cool*.

Even though some of the outfits felt far too wild for me, I ended up buying most of the things Max said *I just had to have!* But I didn't need persuading to buy the boots. They were this yummy shade of pink – you know, almost good enough to eat – soft leather with tassels and things. As soon as I put them on I felt as if they were meant to be mine. I sat in the shoe shop, with my feet sticking out in front of me, and I just started to smile. In those boots, I almost believed I *could* be a completely different person. I couldn't bear to take them off, so Max asked the salesgirl if she'd spray them with that protector stuff, so I could wear them home.

On the bus back we had to have a seat each because we'd got so many bags between us. I kept sneaking looks down at my boots. I knew my mum would never have let me buy them. She'd have said they were far too expensive – and too grown up for me – and too flashy and too...lots of other things. I wondered for a moment what she'd do when she found out about my spending spree, but I pushed that to the back of my mind.

When we got home, Auntie Paula was in the

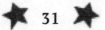

middle of cooking the supper and Uncle Dougie was listening to the football results. When they found out we'd spent a hundred and fifty pounds, Auntie Paula blew up like a tornado all over again. Only this time she blew right off the scale. Luckily for me, she blamed everything on Max. Luckily for Max, she took most of her temper out on the pots and pans and the kitchen cupboard doors.

'My God! *Bang!* What has got into you Maxine?! *Clatter!* Have you completely lost your mind?! *Crash!* What on Earth is going on here?!'

Uncle Dougie said he'd just remembered a job he had to do on his car and made a quick getaway. Chip put his head round the kitchen door to see what all the yelling was about, but ducked right out again when he saw his mum waving a big frying-pan around. Max grabbed me and all my bags and told me we should probably escape upstairs as well, just 'till things blew over.

'Don't think you've heard the last of this, *Maxine,*' Auntie Paula called after us. 'I shall want a full explanation. And mark my words, Heads Will Roll!'

I must have looked as scared as I felt, because Max said, 'Oh, for goodness sake, you're such a worrier, Izzy. Do something with your face, before you trip over it. I told you before, Mum'll come round. And when she does, we'll have a fashion show. It's gonna be fine, trust me.'

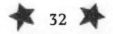

Then my super-scary fairy godmother stopped being quite so scary for a minute. She lay back on her bed, as if absolutely nothing had happened, reading her magazines – cool as a cucumber. No, cooler than that. Cool as an ice-cube!

I'd never met anyone like Max before. And suddenly I wanted to be just like her.

six

I was getting used to Max always turning out to be right. By the time we'd had supper, and I'd helped to clear away again, Auntie Paula's temper had pretty well blown itself out.

'You are a sweetheart to help,' she said. 'OK, let's have this fashion show.'

I got quite excited, trying all my new clothes on again, because each time I put them on they felt a *little* more like 'me'.

Uncle Dougie was trying to join in and be nice. But when he said I looked *funky* and *groovy*, Max begged him to stop embarrassing everyone.

I showed them the skirts, the cropped jeans, the skinny tops and matching tights. Auntie Paula told me my mum had worn tights just like mine when she was my age. I couldn't believe that. Auntie Paula, maybe, but not my mum – unless she was very different when she was young.

Auntie Paula finally had to admit that they were all very nice. 'Nothing too extreme, thankfully,' she said.

Until we got to the boots...

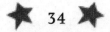

'Oh, Max, it's the summer term. Boots, for goodness sake!'

Max shook her head sadly. 'Mum, you really have no idea, do you? Leave it to those who do.'

But Auntie Paula was most worried about the money. 'I don't know what I'm going to tell my poor sister. As if she hasn't got enough on her plate.'

'Then don't tell Auntie Lynda anything,' said Max. 'It's Isabella's money. It's up to her how she spends it! She's twelve, for goodness sake, not a baby.'

I was standing in the kitchen, while Max and her mum argued about me as if I wasn't even there. Suddenly, Auntie Paula must have realised because she came over and gave me another big hug.

'As if you haven't got enough to deal with,' she said. 'I hold Max entirely responsible for this. None of it's your fault, Isabella. Don't worry, I'll sort things with your mum. And take no notice of Max, her school's not that scary.'

'That's how much you know,' Max muttered.

'Anyway, Chip'll be in your class,' Auntie Paula told me. 'He'll look out for you.'

Max burst out laughing. 'And this is meant to cheer her up?'

Even Auntie Paula smiled then. 'Anyway, Max, I'm going to let this go, now, as long as you

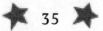

promise me there'll be no more surprises. Because, to be honest, I don't think your dad can handle the stress.'

We all looked over at Uncle Dougie, who'd fallen asleep during the fashion show, and was sitting bolt upright on a kitchen chair, snoring softly.

'My dad could sleep anywhere,' Max said, shaking her head, 'anytime, night or day. In fact, if he was any more laid back he'd be a Lilo.'

'I heard that,' said Uncle Dougie, without a flicker. 'For your information I'm not asleep, just resting my eyes.'

Later on, Max offered to make room in her wardrobe for my new clothes, but she let me hang them on the doors instead, so that I could see them even when I went to bed. I put my precious boots *under* the bed where I could reach them if I wanted to.

When Mum rang later it was really awkward again. The day before I'd felt too miserable to talk to her, now I had to be really careful I didn't give myself away. I didn't dare tell Mum about my hair, or the shopping, not yet. When she'd been to the hospital and got all the tests out of the way Auntie Paula said that perhaps then she'd tell her. But I wasn't used to having secrets from my mum, so when she asked what I'd been up to, I sort of muttered, 'Oh, not much. Just mooched around town a bit with Max,' and got off the phone as quickly as I could.

Before Max turned her light out that evening, she sat up in bed filling in a questionnaire in one of her magazines.

'Listen to this,' she said. 'If you heard a rumour that your boyfriend had been cheating on you, would you:

'A) Give him the benefit of the doubt until you'd checked it out.

'B) Tell him you don't go out with people you can't trust.

'C) Tell him to sling his hook and find some other bimbo.

'Or, better still,' said Max, 'make photocopies of his ugly mug and stick them all over school with the caption: Liar, Liar, pants on fire!'

When Max asked me if I had a boyfriend yet, I went a bit red. Dawn and me don't really know any boys of our own age, even the ones at school make us nervous. Dawn's my best friend, my only friend really. She's got a brother, called Robbie, but he's just a pest. We call him *Little Turd* – when her mum's not around.

I loved lying in bed, listening to Max reading things out of her magazine, even if some of them were a bit embarrassing. It was like having a big sister of my own. I've always wished there was

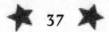

someone else in my family, apart from me and Mum. I've never had a dad. Well, I know I must have done once, but I've never met him. And Mum won't talk about him, even when I ask her.

Mum doesn't talk a lot really. She says she's a very private person. She has friends at work, but not close friends. And she's never very keen on me having friends round to tea, or having Dawn to sleep over. Even before she was ill, on weekdays Mum was always too tired after work. And at weekends, she always said, she liked our routines, just the two of us: food shopping and going into town on Saturdays, then cleaning and catching up with TV soaps on Sundays.

Once Mum told me she was glad I'd got Dawn, because it's nice to have friends. But, she said, it's just as important to be independent. That way you don't get let down. Besides, as long as we've got each other, why would we need anybody else? It only takes two to make a family. Well, that's what Mum said.

After Max turned the light off, she bombarded me with more questions, but it wasn't scary like it was when I first arrived, because now we were lying in the dark and I didn't feel so shy. Max said it was a relief to find I could actually string together an interesting sentence or two. I think that was meant to be a compliment.

When Max asked me about my dad, I told her I

didn't know very much, just the little bits Mum had told me – that they'd been far too young and it had all been a big mistake, though she always adds, that doesn't mean *I* was a mistake. *I* am the best thing in her life, she says.

Max couldn't believe I didn't know *anything* about my dad apart from his name: Will Sutton.

I said, 'Mum doesn't like talking about it.'

'So?! Don't you think you've got a right to know?' Max asked me.

I wasn't sure. I hadn't thought about it like that.

'Doesn't it make you angry? If I were you I'd stamp and shout 'till I found out.'

I told Max that I didn't do much stamping and shouting. Max said that was probably one of the things that was wrong with me. I wasn't sure what she meant by that. Anyway, she said she didn't really believe me. She said, '*Everyone* gets mad. Even you must lose your temper, sometimes.'

But I didn't usually. Really, I didn't.

Of course Mum makes me mad a lot of the time, with the way she fusses about the house being neat and tidy and having everything just the way *she* wants it. That's why I spend so much time in my bedroom, I can please myself there. But I try not to fall out with Mum because if ever I do she gets upset and starts to cry and I hate to see her upset. And when she starts to say it must be her fault, and what a bad mother she is, I end up

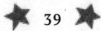

having to cheer *her* up. 'It never seems worth it,' I told Max.

'It's always worth it,' said Max. 'You need to toughen up, girl. Get in touch with your wild side.'

I said I wasn't sure I had one, but Max said not to worry, if I had, she'd find it. We weren't finished yet. We'd only had Phases One and Two.

'This isn't only about hair and clothes, you know,' she told me. 'We're going for The Full Works, remember? The complete package.'

I *still* didn't know what that meant. I lay in the dark, imagining myself like a parcel. You know what it's like sometimes when you get a present that looks really exciting, wrapped in shiny paper and ribbon with curly ends, but when you open it, the wrapping turns out to be the best part of it.

I was worried I'd be like that. My scary fairy godmother might be able to make me look cool and exciting on the outside but when people actually got to know *me* – boring, shy Bella – I'd just be a big disappointment. I knew it was going to take more than a new hairstyle and clothes to turn mousey-me into someone like Max. Someone who was cool and funny, who could stamp and shout and get her own way. That would take *real* magic.

Max had gone quiet and I thought she must be asleep, so it felt safe to reach under my bed and

lift my boots out of the box. I was just sniffing the new leather when Max said, 'They smell great, don't they, new boots?'

I felt a bit stupid, but I grinned. You couldn't get anything past Max.

'So what do your friends call you?' she asked. 'Isabella sounds a bit…Sunday-tea-time-mind-your-manners. Don't you have a nickname?'

'Um, my best friend, Dawn, sometimes calls me Ellie-bellie,' I said.

Max grunted. She wasn't impressed with that.

'Mum calls me Bella,' I said, 'when she's in a good mood.'

'Bella's an OK name…for a *dog!*' Max said. 'No, what you need is a new cool name to go with your new cool image. What about…Izzy? How does that grab you?'

I lay in the dark, trying the name out in my head.

Izzy. It's Izzy here. Hi, my name's Izzy.

I loved it. I wasn't sure if I could ever live up to it – or my new hairstyle – or my new clothes. All of them felt super-scary, but I loved them even so. I reached down and stroked my new boots again. Then I lay awake for ages, wondering how on earth I would manage to carry it all off and not let my new scary fairy godmother down.

seven

It was nine o'clock when I woke up on Sunday morning, and Max was already back in scary fairy godmother mode.

She was on her mobile. First she seemed to be talking to Leah, but then she went on to make lots more calls. She kept talking about someone called Izzy and I got this sick feeling in my stomach when I suddenly remembered that was me! The more I overheard, the further down the bed I wanted to slide. I couldn't believe the lies she was telling people about me.

'Tell Amber to watch out for my cousin in school tomorrow. She'll be well-jealous when she sees her. Izzy's got the looks and the gear. She's seriously classy! A bit like me, really! Ha, ha!'

'I've got my cousin Izzy staying here for a bit. I bet when your Hayley meets her they'll be joined at the hip. She's wicked. She'll do anything for a laugh.'

I had no idea what Max was up to. I kept shaking my head, trying to get her attention, but she just ignored me. What was she doing?! That didn't sound anything like me. And no one was

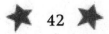

going to believe any of it – not once they met me. How would I ever dare show my face at that school now?

'Hiya. My cousin Izzy's staying. She's gonna be in Beccy's class. Tell her to watch out, Izzy might seem like butter-wouldn't-melt, at first, but believe me, Beccy definitely doesn't want to mess with her. She's a bit…wild.'

When Max finally switched off her phone, she was looking pretty pleased with herself. There was a big grin across her face.

'OK, hon,' she said. 'That's Phase Three started. Now you've got a reputation, you'd better live up to it. Don't let me down.'

I felt so mad with Max, I wanted to ask her what on earth she thought she was playing at, stamp and shout even. But, as usual, I didn't. I wimped out and hid behind my quilt, feeling ill, hoping it might turn into flu, or something worse that would save me from having to go to school tomorrow.

Leah came round after breakfast so Max made me do another fashion show. After Leah had given everything her approval, she and Max decided exactly what I should wear for school the next day. They chose the black mini-skirt and picked some striped tights to go with it and a top which was exactly the same colour as the stripes in my hair. And my boots of course! It didn't look like

any kind of uniform I'd have got away with at my old school. But I did feel kind of good in it, although it still didn't stop the sick feeling in my stomach at the thought of my first day at Max's school.

Max and Leah went through everyone they'd rung, which sounded like most of the people in my new class. But Max said, 'No, just the movers and shakers.'

'Why would anyone bother with the boys?' asked Leah.

'They're mostly neanderthals like Chip,' Max agreed.

Even so, Leah pointed out, perhaps they ought to put Chip in the picture. But even after Max had explained it three times to him, Chip still looked blank.

'OK, one last time,' she said. 'You've got this dead-cool cousin, Izzy, who's staying here for a while. She may seem quiet – at first – but really she's wild, off the wall. Small, but deadly, right?'

Chip looked at Max as if *she* was off the wall.

He said, 'Izzy? Who's Izzy? Do I know this person?'

'Aarrgh! I've already told you, you're looking at her, dummy,' Max almost screamed. 'Now, remember, she's the hottest new kid in school.'

Chip looked me up and down, then he burst out laughing. That was it. Any tiny hope I might have

had of fooling anyone disappeared into thin air.

Max gave Chip a withering look and warned him what horrible fate awaited him if he blew things for me. Then she told me to ignore him. She said, 'Chip wouldn't recognise style if it tripped him up and mugged him.'

'Not even then,' agreed Leah.

'Anyway,' Max said, 'if I have to, I'll pay him to keep quiet.'

'You usually do,' said Leah. 'Your brother should have, *What's it Worth?* tattooed on his forehead.'

For the rest of the day, whatever I said and did, Max was on my case.

'This is all part of Phase Three,' she told me.

I had to stand up for myself – smile a bit more – not stare into my food whenever anyone asked me a question. When Auntie Paula gave me pudding, even after I'd said, no thanks, and I politely started to eat it, Max said, 'You see?! This is what I'm talking about. You've got to know what you want, Izzy. If you mean *no* say *no* and then keep on saying it 'till people listen.'

Auntie Paula told her several times to leave me alone. Uncle Dougie said that surely one assertive teenager was enough in any house and Chip said it was *more* than enough. But Max didn't let up. She even told me off about skulking

around with my head down, which is just the way I walk.

'If you're gonna carry "Izzy" off,' she told me, 'you're gonna have to get your head into gear.'

But there seemed to be so much to think about, by the end of the day my head didn't feel in gear so much as in overdrive.

Mum had been ringing around seven o'clock each evening, but when it got to nine o'clock and I was ready to go to bed she still hadn't called. Auntie Paula suggested we give her a ring instead.

'She might be feeling a little bit anxious,' she said.

For a minute I couldn't think why. Then, when I remembered, I felt really bad. What with the makeover, and the shopping, and trying to take in everything Max was throwing at me, and being so worried about my first day at the new school, everything about home had gone out of my head. I'd totally forgotten that Mum was going into hospital for her tests tomorrow.

I couldn't believe it was only three days since I'd been back at home with her. So much had happened already and somehow my new life at Max's, however scary and unreal, actually felt more real than my *real* life. How could that be?

I was feeling really bad about all the things I hadn't told Mum. And when I did get to talk to her

I had to keep on pretending everything was normal, but I could tell that Mum was pretending as well – pretending not to be upset.

'Oh, I'm fine, darling, my case is all packed. I've booked a taxi to the hospital. Don't you worry about me. But, how are you doing? Are you excited about your first day at school? Tell me everything you've been up to today.'

Apart from the things I couldn't tell her, there didn't seem much left to talk about, so as soon as I could I passed the phone over to Auntie Paula again. The amount of laughing and chatting they were doing every time they got on the phone together, you wouldn't have guessed that before Mum got ill they hardly spoke to each other.

Afterwards, Auntie Paula came to find me. 'How are you feeling, Izzy? Max tells me that's what you want us to call you now.'

I smiled and shrugged.

'You know it's going to turn out to be nothing, don't you? Between you and me, your mum's always been a bit of a worrier. I used to tell her she could worry for England. I'm sure the reason she's tired and run down is because she's always doing too much. She just doesn't know how to relax. That's all that's wrong with her.'

Soon after that, even though it was still early, I went up and got into bed. I was thinking about Mum and what Auntie Paula had said. She was

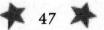

right about Mum always worrying too much. I suppose that's where I get it from. And Mum definitely does too much, even though I do lots to help her around the house. Perhaps a few days rest in hospital was all she needed.

I was also worrying about school tomorrow. But I didn't want Max to see that, so I was hiding behind one of her magazines in bed, pretending to read, when she came upstairs.

'Are you ready for the big day?' she asked.

'I'm feeling a bit nervous,' I admitted – which was an understatement.

But how could I tell my scary fairy godmother that even the thought of the new school and meeting all those new kids wasn't scaring me half as much as trying to live up to the new image she'd given me?

Max said there was no point telling me not to be nervous – Rowan Park was a *big* school – there were some tough kids in it. But if I remembered everything she'd been telling me, it'd be a piece of cake.

I must have looked like I didn't really believe her, because she said, 'OK, there are one or two crucial rules for surviving school. First of all it's about *looking cool* – which we've already taken care of: you've got the hair, you've got the gear and you've got a cool name now.

'Tomorrow it's all down to you. Like I've been

telling you: head up, boobs out. You've gotta walk-the-walk, talk-the-talk – and act the part – not like you own the place, you know, but like you've got a right to be there.

'But most important of all,' she said, looking me straight in the eye, 'choose your friends carefully. That way you'll keep out of trouble, 'cos trouble's for mugs – M-U-G-S,' Max spelled it out for me, in case I was completely stupid, 'and, trust me, Izzy, mugs are not COOL.'

I didn't know how I was going to manage even half of it, but Max hadn't finished yet. She told me the main thing was to *believe* in the new me, 'cos, if *I* didn't, no one else would.

'From now on it's up to you, kiddo. But don't worry, it's not like we're trying to turn you from…*a pumpkin*, into something else entirely,' she said. 'We're just giving you the chance to improve on a few little things about yourself, right?'

I nodded. I didn't dare do anything else.

'Wouldn't you like to be a bit braver, a bit cooler, a bit more popular?' she asked. 'Wouldn't you like to have a bit more fun? You've heard of *fun*, right?'

I smiled and nodded again.

'That's good,' she said, ''cos I was beginning to wonder. OK, better get some sleep now. Got a big day tomorrow.'

'OK. Goodnight, Max,' I said.

When I turned off the light, my head was bursting with everything Max had told me. I was terrified I was going to let her down and then what would she say if I did? While I was asleep, I hoped Max might sprinkle me with some mega-magic scary fairy dust. Then maybe, just maybe, I might pull it off. Because without it, I didn't have a chance.

eight

The next morning, Max walked me as far as the main entrance to Rowan Park High School. It was in three different buildings. It made my school look like a tiddly, little primary school. You couldn't see much inside because the windows were so high, but the front doors were wide open and a huge stream of kids was disappearing inside. Even the kids looked bigger than at my school.

I must have had a pathetic look on my face because Max said, 'No way, kiddo. You can surely find your own way to the classroom.'

Before she went off to her own building, she pointed me in the right direction and left me to walk down the long corridors alone.

It wasn't my imagination – everyone *was* staring at me. I didn't know if it was because of my clothes – I'd told Max the skirt was too short, I had to keep tugging it down. Or because of my hair – I still wasn't used to the way some of it was straight and the rest was kinky and the fringe hung in my eyes. Or it could have been because

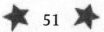 51

people *always* stare at you when you're new.

When I finally reached the classroom there were a couple of girls waiting outside, leaning against the wall. The minute they saw me coming, they raced inside and, right down the corridor, I could hear their voices as clear as anything:

'Look out! She's here! The new kid's here!'

'Oh, my God! Wait 'till you see her!'

I could feel my breakfast, what little bit I'd eaten, sitting in my stomach, threatening to come back. When I got to the classroom door I could see small groups of kids sitting on table tops and window ledges and every one of them was staring at me – apart from Chip and Danny, who were pretending they didn't know me, and weren't in the least bit interested in doing so.

I tried to remember any one of Max's tips. I tried to remember what she'd told people about me. I tried to stop my brain going into panic-overdrive. I thought about turning round and running back down the corridor – all two hundred miles home to my mum. But my legs didn't feel as if they'd carry me into the room, never mind back down the corridor. So I stood there instead, shaking and thinking, help, Help! HELP!

But I needn't have worried. Suddenly a group of the girls crowded round me – grabbing me by my arms – and almost carried me inside.

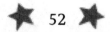 52

'Hi, Izzy. I'm Hayley, this is Lauren and Amber.'

'We're Beccy, Naomi, Jacquette and...'

'Ruth. Hi! Love your hair – it's fab. I could eat it.'

'Take no notice of Ruth, she's potty.'

'Great boots, great skirt.'

'Don't crowd the girl,' said Hayley. I could see she was the one in charge. 'Max said you were dead class. We love your cousin. She's so cool.'

Then Mr Hathaway, the form teacher, came in and told everyone to park their bums while he took the register. No one seemed to think it was odd, except me. None of the teachers at my school would ever use the word *bum*.

Hayley and Amber tried to pull me over to sit by them, but Beccy and Naomi wouldn't let go of my other arm.

'Try to leave the poor girl in one piece, would you,' Mr Hathaway told them, 'at least until breaktime?'

There was a spare seat by Ruth so Mr Hathaway told me to sit in it. Ruth did this victory wave, like she'd won the lottery. Nobody's ever wanted to sit by *me* that much before – apart from Dawn. I couldn't believe it but I thought, might as well enjoy it while it lasts. I couldn't wait to write and tell Dawn. Even some of the boys were looking over and grinning at me.

'Just ignore them,' Ruth whispered. 'They're all bozos, apart from Damian de Blanc, of course.'

 53

She pointed to a tall boy behind us with dark hair and quite brown skin, dressed all in white. 'He's quite new here as well. His dad's French,' she told me. 'Everyone thinks Damian's really dishy.'

As I turned to look where she was pointing, he caught me looking straight at him. My face went as pink as my hair. I was so embarrassed because, like I said, I've always been really nervous of boys. I didn't say anything to Ruth, but when Damian smiled at me and showed all these lovely white teeth I could see she was right, he *was* dishy.

By the end of the day, loads of people had come over to speak to me. But it wasn't too scary because wherever I went, I was surrounded by a gang of girls telling me who everyone was and how everything worked, and admiring how I looked, and firing questions at me. I tried to do as Max had told me: walk-the-walk, stand up straight, look people in the eye, even though, inside, I wanted to curl up in a corner. I'd always been so shy, especially when I first met anyone, but no one was leaving any room for me to be shy. It was full-on.

Any time it got difficult, and they asked questions about my life at home with Mum, I went quiet and started to freeze up, like Bella would have done. But then Hayley would save me, 'Cool it, you lot. Let Izzy get her breath.'

I had to keep reminding myself that was who I was supposed to be – Izzy. Not Bella, definitely not her, but this cool kid, who made people laugh every time she spoke.

'You're hilarious,' Ruth said one time when somebody asked me how I got to be so cool, and I said she'd have to ask my scary fairy godmother. Only I wasn't joking.

The only people who were keeping their distance were the two coolest looking girls in my class, Cassie and Danielle. They both had black hair tied back tight against their heads with long, wispy curls hanging down at the front and big gold earrings. They wore crop tops and jogging bottoms and trainers. They looked older than everyone else. I'd seen them give me sideways looks to begin with, but even they seemed impressed when some year ten girls – friends of Max's – came to ask me how it was going.

Later, between lessons, Cassie and Danielle came and leaned against each other by my desk and introduced themselves.

'Those boots are well-cool,' said Cassie. 'Let's try 'em on.'

I was a bit surprised but I didn't know what else to do so I handed one over. I was quite glad when Cassie couldn't get it on, even though she tried hard enough.

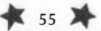

'They're not going to fit you,' Hayley told her. 'Your feet are too big.'

Cassie just narrowed her eyes and looked at Hayley for a long minute before she said, 'Everything about me's big, I thought you knew that – larger than life and twice as scary.'

Hayley didn't say anything back. She went really pink. After that Cassie ignored her. She handed me my boot back and smiled at me. 'See you around, Boots.'

After she'd gone Hayley said, 'You watch, she'll have a pair tomorrow.'

Later, I asked Ruth why Hayley and Cassie didn't seem to like each other. Ruth rolled her eyes and said, 'Hayley and Danielle *used* to be best friends,' as if that explained everything.

But it wasn't only Hayley that seemed nervous of Cassie, all the girls did. And she was scary. Not scary like Max, different kind of scary. The way she talked to the teachers! Like she couldn't be bothered to answer their questions. But she could make everyone in the class laugh. She was always making jokes and doing crazy things. It was right what she'd said about herself, she was larger than life. As well as scary.

At the end of the day, Hayley and Lauren said they'd walk me home because they only lived round the corner from Max. But in the end there were about six of them who wanted to show me the short cuts and where the shops were.

There were two boys from our class as well, walking on the other side of the road, making silly jokes, trying to get us to notice them. Their names were Brad and Dipak, but everyone called them Betty and Doris. Lauren told me I didn't have to worry about those two, they were perfectly harmless.

When we reached Max's house, Hayley said they'd come and call for me in the morning before school. Then they all stood at the gate, waving and saying, 'By-y-y-e,' as if they weren't going to see me for a month.

I'd never been this popular before. I couldn't believe I'd managed not to give myself away for a whole day. It had been exciting but nerve-wracking too. But I didn't know how much longer I could hide the fact I wasn't a bit like the person they thought I was.

Then what would happen?

nine

'OK. Don't leave anything out,' Max told me when she got in from school – before she even got her jacket off. 'I want all the grisly details. *Everything*.'

But actually there weren't any *grisly* details; I'd had a fantastic day really. It had been exhausting, trying to remember everything she'd told me and pretending to be someone I wasn't. And scary – worrying whether I'd get caught out. But, even so – and even though I knew it couldn't last – it had probably been the best day at school in my entire life.

I told Max, 'Everyone liked my hair. And my clothes. And my boots!'

She said, 'Obviously, they recognise style when they see it.'

'And I think I remembered all the rules,' I told her. 'I hung out with Hayley and Amber and lots of their friends. They all brought me home.'

'Sounds like you did me proud, girl. Now, you've gotta keep up the good work. Don't let us both down.'

But Max wasn't quite so pleased when Chip told

her about Cassie trying my boots on and chatting to me. I thought, for someone who didn't seem interested in anything but computers, Chip didn't miss much.

Max said, 'Sounds like you forgot the most important rule. I'm telling you, Izzy: keep well away from her. Cassie McCloud's T-R-O-U-B-L-E, and trouble is for…?'

'Mugs,' I grinned at her.

'Right,' she said. 'And this time don't forget.'

I felt like telling Max she had nothing to worry about. I'd never been in trouble in my life. Well, apart from the one time when Dawn and I had a big fall-out because she spilled a bottle of milk over my Vikings project that I'd just got my best ever mark for. We didn't speak to each other for a week, until Mrs Hollbeck threatened us both with a detention for being so silly. We made it up there and then, because neither of us wanted a detention.

After supper, I was emptying the dishwasher for Auntie Paula, when Mum rang. Before she handed me the phone, Auntie Paula told Mum she didn't know how she'd managed before I came. She said how nice it was, having a little helper for a change.

Mum was pleased about that. She asked me how my first day at school had gone. I told her it had

been absolutely great. And how different the school was to mine, how much friendlier the teachers were, more laid back and jokey. Even the dinners were better. I had so much more to tell Mum I almost forgot she was ringing from the hospital.

When I remembered to ask her how it had gone, she said, 'Oh, OK. They've done lots of tests today. And there'll be more tomorrow. I won't get the results for a couple of weeks, though. Anyway, sweetheart, I won't talk much longer, I'm feeling a bit tired. In fact, considering I've done nothing, I'm exhausted. But I'm glad school wasn't too bad.'

Not too bad! It was brilliant! And it was all thanks to Max, my scary fairy godmother who, now I was getting used to her, didn't feel quite so scary. In fact, I thought – apart from Mum being ill – if I could just keep it up, things couldn't *be* any better.

But I was wrong. From then on things kept on getting better and better.

For the next two weeks it didn't feel like going to school. In fact, it was like Max had said: more like having fun. I hadn't *hated* going to my old school, but it wasn't *fun*. Now I couldn't wait for the doorbell to ring every morning. All the way to school it was chat, chat, chat.

There'd usually be a few boys not far behind,

calling after us, making rude remarks. Then we'd try to work out who fancied who.

One time Hayley said, 'Half the boys in our class fancy *you*.'

I went bright pink and shook my head. But everyone seemed to think I was just pretending.

'You can't fool us. We've heard all about you!'

'And your reputation!'

So when they pressed me about whether I had a boyfriend at my old school, I found myself saying, 'Maybe. One or two.' I chose the two most popular boys in my class to tell them about. I thought, why not, no one's ever going to know. It was the first real lie I'd told. I was surprised how easy it felt. After a while I almost started to believe it myself. It was like Max had said, if I believed it – if I talked the talk – everyone else would believe me. And they did.

'I knew it!' said Hayley. 'I told you she probably had loads of boys after her?'

Amber nodded. 'My mum says it's always the quiet ones.'

'Always the quiet ones...what?' Ruth asked.

'That get the boys, dummy,' said Lauren.

It was funny the way people talked about me, as if I wasn't there. It didn't bother me, in fact I'd started to wear this little smile whenever they did, like I knew something they didn't. Which was true, after all. And it meant that whenever I was

still a bit quiet at school, it wasn't a problem. In fact everyone seemed to think it meant I was *a bit deep*, like I was weighing things up, waiting for my moment. Maybe, if I was careful, I thought, I might not give myself away after all. And it was only for two weeks.

Sometimes, boys from my class would come and sit on my desk in between lessons. Betty and Doris were OK, they just made me laugh. But some of the others really teased me. I tried not to blush, because I knew that Max, my now not-so-scary fairy godmother, would tell me blushing definitely wasn't cool. And I hardly ever said anything back to any of them – that would have been way too scary – but instead of looking down at the floor, like Bella would have done, Izzy managed to look them straight in the eye at least and it was as if suddenly they thought *I* was the scary one.

'Whoa! See that look?'

'Better watch out what you say to her, man.'

'Haven't you heard? She's a bit wild.'

One day, a folded up message landed on my desk. It was from someone asking me to go out with them. I stuffed it in my bag, quickly, before anyone saw it. Whoever wrote it had forgotten to sign it. So, thank goodness, I didn't have to take any notice of that.

ten

I was really getting used to living at the Ross's. With Auntie Paula so laid back, compared to my mum, I was enjoying being able to please myself a bit more.

Auntie Paula was so busy, working as a midwife, that often when we got home from school there'd be a message on the kitchen table telling us that our dinner was in the oven, or the fridge, because one of her pregnant mums was about to *drop her baby*. The first time I read that I must have looked a bit shocked because Max said, 'That's nothing. I've heard far worse than that while I was growing up. I hold my mum entirely responsible for putting me off having babies for life!'

Uncle Dougie's a driving instructor, he often works in the evenings and weekends too. So a lot of the time Max and Chip and me had the house to ourselves. After his homework, if he did any, Chip was usually on his computer. Max was always teasing him about the unhealthy relationship he had with it. She said she dreaded to think what sites he surfed. Any day she expected the Vice

Squad to come knocking on their door.

Chip was used to being teased by the whole family. Now I was there he seemed pleased to get his own back. His favourite trick was messing up my hair. I didn't mind. I was getting used to being teased now. Mostly he teased me about Betty and Doris who he said had a thing about me. I asked him why everyone called them that.

'Because they're like a pair of girls,' he said, 'always gossiping.'

'What d'you mean?' I rounded on him. 'You've got some nerve. Nobody gossips more than you and Fishy.'

'Fishy?!' Chip almost squealed. 'No one calls Danny *Fishy*.'

'I do,' I said. If other people could tease me, why shouldn't I do the same back I suddenly decided?

Chip blinked. 'When did you get to be so cheeky?' he said. I grinned. I liked being cheeky for a change. Anyway, Chip said, getting back to Betty and Doris, did I realise they'd got my name written all over their English books?

I said, 'Don't be so silly.' But it did make me wonder if it was one of those two that had sent me the anonymous note at school.

And then there were the phonecalls. More and more friends were ringing me, which meant I was practically on the phone all evening. At first Max treated it all as a great joke, and teased me about

how Cinderella had been to the ball and turned into Princess Popularity. But then she started to seem a bit irritated by it, especially when she wanted to save money on her mobile by talking to Leah on her mum and dad's phone and I was already on it.

One day she came home and found a whole gang of us sitting on the garden wall fooling about. She complained all evening about how our bags had been littering the path so that she could hardly get into her own house. Suddenly, she seemed a bit fed up with having me, and all my friends, hanging around. But how could that be? Wasn't this exactly what Max had planned in the first place?

She *really* didn't like it the first time Cassie McCloud called, though. I was as surprised as Max when she rang – I'd hardly spoken more than two words to her at school – she asked if I wanted to meet her and Danielle down the park. I didn't even go, but Max still got mad with me.

'I thought I warned you about *her*,' she said.

I didn't want to argue with Max but I couldn't understand why she had such a thing about Cassie. To be honest, I thought Cassie was a bit like Max – so cool she was almost scary – but I knew better than to say that. The fact that nothing and no one scared Cassie was the thing I admired most about her. As well as the way you

never knew what she was going to say or do next. I wanted to be more like that. I didn't want to be nervous and shy and scared, like Bella, any more. I wanted to feel more like the Izzy I was pretending to be.

At my old school, Dawn and me had always kept well away from girls like Cassie and Danielle. Not that girls like them would ever have been interested in us either. We'd have been far too boring – I could see that as soon as I got Dawn's first letter. Even though she was still my best friend, I felt embarrassed when I read it, especially the way it started: *Hi Ellie-bellie.*

Oh, yuk. I could just imagine what Cassie would say if she read that!

The letter itself was just about teachers at school and the boring homework they'd set us to do in history and French and every other boring lesson. And what her revolting little brother had been up to. I did try a few times to write back, but in the end I always screwed it up and threw it away.

I didn't know how to start to tell Dawn about everything that had happened in the short time since I'd seen her. I still wanted to be friends with her, but I couldn't find a way to tell her that I didn't want her to call me Ellie-bellie any more. I hated that silly name! I was Izzy now.

My new name caused a big argument with Mum too. One night when she rang, Max called me:

'Izzy, Izzy, phone for you! It's your mum.'

I could tell Mum was in a bit of a strop as soon as I heard her voice.

'Why on earth is Maxine calling you that horrible nickname?'

'It's not horrible, Mum,' I told her. 'I like it.'

'It's so ugly and silly. What's the point of me giving you a lovely name like Isabella if you're going to let people turn it into a stupid name like that?'

'I *like* it,' I said again, even sharper this time.

'I don't know what's got into you, Bella. Usually you—' Mum started, but I cut her off.

'Auntie Paula's here,' I said, handing over the phone.

Auntie Paula must have overheard, or Mum must have been going on to her too, because later she came and put her arm round me and reminded me that Mum still hadn't had the results of her tests.

'She's bound to be feeling a bit anxious,' she said. 'This is a difficult time for both of you.'

I nodded. Of course I felt sorry for my mum, and I was worried about her, but sometimes I couldn't help feeling cross with her. Now I felt guilty for showing it, though. I hardly ever snapped at Mum like that.

Later on, when Max came upstairs, she came and sat on my bed. I could tell Auntie Paula

had been talking to her.

'You mustn't worry about your mum, you know,' she said. 'Mum says everything's going to turn out OK. She's sure it's a false alarm.'

I wanted to believe that, more than anything in the world. But I didn't tell Max that just then that wasn't what I'd been thinking about. I was still thinking about the stupid argument over my name.

I really wanted Mum to understand that Izzy felt more than a nickname to me now. It felt like the person I wanted to be. I *looked* like Izzy. And I was starting – sometimes at least – to feel like Izzy. Surely it was up to me, wasn't it? It was my name after all!

eleven

Why is it that when you're really having fun, time seems to go by so much faster? Those first two weeks at Max's flew by and when they were almost up I started to wish...well, not that Mum would be ill a bit longer, *of course, not that*, only that she might need a little more time to get over her tests so I could stay – just for another week. Or maybe two.

Hayley had asked me to tea the following week and Amber had invited me to her birthday sleepover in a few weeks' time. When I told them that by then I'd probably have gone back home they were both really disappointed. But not as disappointed as I was.

Max wasn't though. I could tell she was more than ready to have her bedroom back to herself. I think she was bored with helping me decide what to wear every day, and doing my hair for me. She hadn't actually said anything, but on Friday morning, when I told her I could probably manage my hair myself that once, she looked pretty relieved. Her mock GCSE's were starting

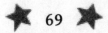

the following week and she said she was way behind with her art project.

'If you're sure,' she said. 'I could do with getting into school early. Have fun.'

I stood in the bedroom after she'd gone and thought, oh, well, this is where it all comes undone. It's probably my last day as Izzy anyway. Next Monday I'll be back at my old school, back to boring Bella and her boring old life, I bet.

I stared at myself in the mirror. I'd watched Max do it enough times. How hard could it be? So I started the *Zig-Zag* routine with the bits of coat hangers and tried not to burn myself on Max's hair straighteners. Of course I did burn myself once or twice, and it took me ages, and the room looked like a bomb had hit it – but I did manage.

OK, so at first I looked like I'd had a bad fright or something – Chip nearly choked on his cereal. 'Mmm,' he said. 'That should scare them off all right.'

But by the time I'd had breakfast it had calmed down a bit and when the doorbell rang everyone told me how great it looked. And the clothes I'd chosen got lots of remarks. It seemed so unfair that just when I was starting to manage without my not-so-scary fairy godmother's help, it was time to go home.

My last day at school was great, though. We spent the afternoon practising for a swimming

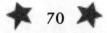

gala that was coming up in a couple of weeks' time and I got to take Jacquette's place because she was off ill. It was lucky it was swimming; it's the only sport I'm any good at.

I swam last in the relay and made up nearly half a length so my team won. Everyone was calling me a star and telling me they were fed up that I wouldn't be there for the actual gala. Even Damian.

'Good job we had you on the team,' he said. 'Now we'll win the shield.'

I don't know where I found the courage to answer him. 'But I won't be here,' I said. 'I go home tomorrow.'

'Pity,' he said and smiled. I almost passed out.

But the other big surprise of the day was when Cassie and Danielle invited me to go into town with them on the weekend!

'You busy tomorrow, Izz? D'you wanna come shopping?'

They asked me, right in front of Hayley and the others, and Hayley really didn't like it. After Cassie had gone, she asked, 'What's *she* up to?' like I'd have any idea. I thought Cassie was just being friendly. Of course, even if I hadn't been going home, I probably wouldn't have gone; I was still nervous of her and Danielle. But it was exciting being asked.

It all seemed so unfair. Half of me wanted to see my mum – I was missing her like mad, and I

wanted to check she was OK. But the other half of me wanted to stay in Manchester and have fun with my new friends.

And both halves weren't looking forward to what Mum would say about the pink bits in my hair. And my new clothes. I wasn't sure when Auntie Paula would get round to telling Mum about all the money I'd spent!

Starting to worry again had me feeling like I was turning back into Bella, and that was something I was really beginning to dread too.

At the end of school everyone wanted to walk me home, to say goodbye. They were all hanging about in the corridor, waiting while I collected some work back from Mr Hathaway. Suddenly, Hayley grabbed me and said, 'I know, let's you and me sneak out the back way, by the Music Block. It'll be a great joke.'

I couldn't see the joke myself but I wasn't in the mood for saying lots of goodbyes so that's what we did. We walked the long route home along the canal towpath and I was thinking how much fun we would've had doing this every day. But just as I was getting to know my way around I had to leave.

It wasn't long before we realised we were being followed. The boys didn't even try to hide. At first Hayley said we should just ignore them, but suddenly she said, 'Come on, let's run.'

We caught them by surprise and left them way behind. But the boys had their bikes and in the end they soon overtook us and stood blocking our path. It was Betty and Doris. They were both red in the face. We were pretty pink too, from running and giggling. Hayley told them to say what they had to say and then scram. Betty nudged Doris, but Doris went even redder and shook his head.

'Oh, for goodness sake, spit it out,' Hayley told them.

So, finally, Betty took a deep breath and managed to talk to us. At least he talked to Hayley, even though it was all about me.

'We want to go out with her,' he said, as if I wasn't even there!

'What, both of you?' said Hayley.

'Yeah. Well, whichever one she chooses. It's up to her.'

'You know she's going home tomorrow,' Hayley reminded them. 'You'll probably never see her again.'

'We could write. E-mail. Text her.'

'Both of you?' said Hayley.

'Yeah. Why not?' said Betty.

I had to bite my lip to stop myself from laughing. It was the most ridiculous thing I'd ever heard.

But it was fun too. I'd never had a boy actually stand there and ask me to go out with him

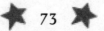

before – now I had two. I couldn't wait to tell Dawn. Brad's small, a bit like a cuddly toy; Dipak's better looking with long, dark, curly eyelashes, but he's as quiet as me. If I went out with him, we'd probably never manage to say a word to each other.

To be honest, I didn't want to go out with anybody. And certainly not either of those two, but I didn't want to hurt their feelings. In the end I said I'd think about it and let them know. They did a high-five and started hugging each other, as if they'd both won a race. Then Hayley and me ran the rest of the way home, screaming with laughter.

I was still giggling when I burst through the kitchen door. I must have been quite pink and out of breath and there was probably a stupid, wide grin all over my face. But that soon disappeared.

Max was home already and so was Auntie Paula. They were standing in the kitchen and I could tell by their faces that something really, really bad had happened. For a minute I went dizzy, I couldn't get my breath. It was like I'd run straight into a brick wall.

twelve

Auntie Paula came over and put her arms around me and made me sit down while she told me the news from the hospital.

'I am so sorry, my darling,' she said, 'but your mum's tests have proved positive.'

My brain couldn't have been working. I didn't understand. Why was Auntie Paula saying she was sorry? Positive was good, wasn't it? But it wasn't.

'It means your mum's got cancer, sweetheart,' Auntie Paula explained. 'A lymphoma.'

I looked blankly at her. What was that?

'It's like leukaemia. It's a blood cancer. That's the reason she's been tired for so long. I know it's hard to take in, but she asked me to explain it to you. But look, it's much better news than it sounds. They've told your mum that, because they've caught it early, she should make a complete recovery.'

I looked up at Auntie Paula, and Max standing behind her. They were both trying to smile, but really they looked like they wanted to cry.

'Anyway,' Auntie Paula went on, 'your mum can't

wait to see you. She's missed you so much. She's out of hospital now so we're still going up tomorrow. But, well, here's the not-so-good news: she's got to have chemotherapy and it's probably going to make her feel quite ill. She'll be in and out of the hospital. I'm afraid that means you'll be coming back here to stay for a bit longer. At least a few more weeks – until she gets over the worst of it. Do you think you can cope with that?'

Max came and put her arm round me. "Course she can. We're roomies now, aren't we? You can put up with me a few more weeks, can't you, babe?'

Max and Auntie Paula were watching me really closely. I think they expected me to start crying. But I didn't. I didn't feel like crying. I didn't *feel* anything. It was like my head was inside a goldfish bowl and everything else was happening outside it. And for a minute or two the only thing I could hear was the sound of the kitchen tap, dripping and hitting the kitchen sink over and over again.

And then it hit me. The thing I'd been wishing for so hard had come true – I wasn't going home after all. I was staying here, with my new friends. It felt like I'd made the whole thing happen and I felt terrible.

When I rang Mum later it was the hardest phone call we'd had yet. I didn't know what to say and every time I tried to tell her how sorry I was, it made her cry, but I knew she didn't understand

what I really meant. The rest of the evening everyone tried so hard to keep me from worrying. Even Chip asked me if I wanted to play computer chess! I almost burst out laughing. I know he was trying to be kind, but *chess*?!

By nine o'clock I was glad to be lying in bed on my own, in the dark. It was too hard to think about my mum having cancer, and being so far away with no one to look after her. I couldn't *bear* to think about that. It was too scary.

I kept telling myself: I want to go back, I want to go back. I didn't mean home. I meant back a few hours – to before I'd heard the bad news, when Damian had smiled at me at school, or to when I'd been coming home and the sun had been shining and I'd been having such a laugh with Hayley.

Hayley had rung after supper to say goodbye all over again. And so had some of the other girls we'd left waiting in the corridor. When I told them I'd be back at school on Monday – I didn't say why, just that there had been a change of plan – they were all excited. Hayley started shrieking down the phone: now I'd be able to come round for tea. And go to Amber's sleepover!

'And,' she said, 'you'd better decide between Betty and Doris before Monday morning. They'll be waiting at the gate when they know.'

I knew she was only teasing me. I mean, no one thought Betty or Doris were a cool catch.

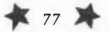

I was still awake when Max came to bed. I didn't want to talk, so I turned to the wall and pretended to be asleep. Max crept about, trying not to wake me. She got into bed and turned her light off straightaway.

I was lying there, thinking about the silly things Betty and Doris had said. I was glad to have something silly to think about. Silly felt safe.

Max must have been able to tell I wasn't asleep yet because she suddenly whispered, 'Are you awake, Izzy?'

I still didn't say anything, and she went quiet again.

No, I thought, I didn't want to go out with Betty or Doris. If it had been Damian, that might have been different. But he was far too dishy to be interested in me. Still, just having him smile at me and say, 'Pity,' was so cool...

I was just drifting off to sleep when Max's voice brought me back. 'Are you OK? Because if you're not, we can talk, you know. It's not a good idea to bottle things up, Izzy.'

I didn't want to talk to Max about my mum, but I couldn't tell her that. And I couldn't talk to her about Damian or Betty and Doris, could I? Although I knew if I did she'd give me some good advice. Max would know what the cool thing was to do. I didn't mean to, but I let out this big sigh.

'It's OK, Izzy,' she whispered. 'You really can talk

to me about anything, you know. Anything at all.'

It sounded as if she meant it. For a moment she didn't sound scary at all. And I did think that Max might be proud of me, having two boys after me. It was all thanks to her. So I took a chance and said, 'Well...there's these two boys in my class, called Betty and Doris...they're not really called Betty and Doris...but, anyway, they both want to go out with me and I don't know what I should say...'

I heard Max sort of gasp and sit up in bed.

'*Izzy!*' she hissed at me. 'I don't believe you. I thought you'd be thinking about your poor mum. Not a couple of nerds from school.'

I wanted to snatch the words back. I felt so stupid. So ashamed. I was glad it was dark and she couldn't see my face burning, or how close I was to crying. I wanted to explain to her, but I was scared I'd only make things worse.

I heard Max drag her quilt back over her and lie down. I knew she must be thinking what a horrible, selfish person I was. And I thought, she's right.

People have always thought that because, as Bella, I was quiet and mousy and shy and never lost my temper or got into trouble, I must be a nice, sweet person. Boring, but nice, and helpful.

But I wasn't. Sometimes I had horrible thoughts in my head. I often felt angry – especially with my mum. I just didn't show it, because I didn't dare

 79

to. I was too scared to upset anyone. Mousy, as well as boring.

Since my fairy godmother's makeover nobody seemed to think I was boring, everyone thought I was funny and trendy and cool. But deep down I'd known it couldn't last. Sooner or later they'd find out about the real me. They'd see how boring I was and, inside, horrible and selfish. Max had already. And now she'd think I didn't even care about my own mum, when I really, really did.

I'd been stupid enough to think that maybe I could become Izzy, if I could only keep on convincing everyone else that that's who I was too.

But now, I realised, that was like believing in fairy tales and *surely*, at twelve, I ought to have grown out of that kind of thing.

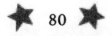

thirteen

I'm not even going to tell you much about that weekend at Mum's, it was too horrible. I've told you how I'd always hated seeing my mum cry, well, she spent most of that weekend crying. But this was much worse because she was crying about having cancer. And about having to go into the hospital for chemotherapy twice a week for the next ten weeks. She was trying to be brave, but she wasn't feeling brave and neither was I.

Mum said that when the women she worked with had found out, one of them had organised a rota of people to take Mum to the hospital. And that made her cry as well. And then, when Auntie Paula said, 'But, Lynda, surely that's what friends are for,' Mum cried all over again.

Auntie Paula was really kind and worked hard, cleaning and shopping and cooking food for Mum to keep her going through the next week. I tried to help as much as I could.

I'd worn my older clothes for the weekend, so that Mum wouldn't find out yet about my new ones, but I don't think it would have mattered.

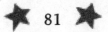 81

With Mum being upset she hardly even mentioned my hair, although she gave me a few funny looks!

She did say at one point that I looked *different*. As if that was a bad thing. But she looked different to me as well – even more tired and really ill now. She looked like someone with cancer and it scared me.

I know it sounds terrible but, even though I didn't want to leave my mum on her own like that, I couldn't wait for the weekend to be over, to get back to Manchester. I couldn't say that and I tried not to show it, but just feeling it made me realise how selfish and horrible I was all over again.

On the journey back in the car, Auntie Paula kept reaching across and squeezing my hand and telling me things would be fine.

She said she felt just terrible about saying that Mum had been worrying over nothing. It clearly hadn't been nothing.

'She's going to get better, though,' she told me. 'I'll make sure of that. We're going to really support her now, you and me. We'll pull her through.'

She tried to cheer us both up by telling funny stories about her and Mum when they were little: how they were always arguing and how Auntie Paula always won because she was the oldest – and the bossiest. Auntie Paula said that was probably one of the reasons why, when Mum ended up a single mum on her own with me, she wouldn't let Auntie Paula help her. She was so determined to prove she could do it alone, she drifted away from her family – even before Grandma and Grandad had died. But now that Mum was ill they were pulling back together because, when things got really bad, that's what families did.

That weekend, seeing Mum and Auntie Paula hugging and crying together, made me wish even more that I had a sister, which reminded me how I'd completely messed things up with Max.

I'd tried not to let my scary fairy godmother down, but somehow I'd managed to and I was worried about seeing her. I wanted to be able to tell her what an idiot I'd been the other night, that I couldn't care less about those stupid boys, I was cooler than that. But I didn't know how to say it and I was scared of making her mad again. So when we got back I was relieved I didn't have to. Max seemed to have got over it all by herself and she asked me lots about how my mum was doing.

Another letter had arrived from Dawn while I'd been at Mum's, telling me she couldn't wait to see me on Monday. She said she had so much to tell me. She didn't know that she wouldn't be seeing

me after all. While I'd been home Mum had suggested I ring Dawn, but I hadn't. I didn't know why. I supposed I felt embarrassed that I hadn't written back to her.

Hayley must have rung round telling everyone that I was staying a bit longer, because there were lots of other messages for me too. I wanted to ring people back but Chip was on the Internet all evening. I tapped on his bedroom door a few times and asked if he was coming off any time this millennium and each time he promised he'd be *finished in five*. But an hour later when he wasn't, I gave up.

Max said, 'Now you can see why I have a mobile. Since Dad's too mean to pay for broadband, how else would I stay in contact with the outside world?'

She looked a bit surprised when I asked her how much a mobile would cost, because I was thinking I might get one. I thought she'd be pleased, after all it was the cool thing to have and everyone else had one – but she said, 'Look, Izzy, perhaps this time you'd better talk it over with your mum before you spend any more money.'

I felt really confused. When I reminded her what she'd said before, about how this was *my* money and I wasn't a baby and I should please myself what I spent it on, she said: 'OK. OK. But things are different now, aren't they?' I didn't know what she expected me to say to that. I just looked at her. 'You're taking things way too far, Izzy,' she snapped. 'Just leave me out of it this time.' Then she walked off.

I knew she'd got into trouble last time, and maybe that was why she was being careful, but I couldn't see what else was bugging her. Anyway, I thought, it *is* my money. Everyone else has got one, so why not me?

Well, if Max didn't want to help me any more, I knew someone else I could ask. I'd heard Cassie McCloud saying that her brother was always getting hold of phones for people. She'd know where I could go for one. I'd ask her tomorrow, if I could get my nerve up.

I decided I wouldn't tell Max that, though. She'd gone back to being pretty scary again – and I wasn't an absolute idiot.

If I'd felt popular before, it was nothing compared to how I felt on Monday morning. Everyone was so pleased to see me back at school, they were falling over me all over again. I noticed that Hayley, and some of the other girls, had started copying what I was wearing. Jacquette had even tried to do her hair like mine, with pink bits as well. It didn't really work. Ruth had got some boots, nice boots, but not as nice as mine. I couldn't wait to tell Max about it, she'd be so

chuffed, I was sure. I thought it might even help get me back in her good books.

When Betty and Doris saw me, they looked like their football team had won the cup. They kept hugging each other. I thought: *idiots!*

But when Damian said, 'So we've gotta put up with you again, have we, Boots?' and smiled his lovely smile at me, I felt like *my* football team had won. And I don't even have one.

Hayley was treating me as if I was her best friend now. She'd sort of dropped Amber so that she could sit by me. Amber had to put up with sharing Hayley with me, but Hayley didn't really like sharing me with anyone else. She especially didn't like it when Cassie McCloud made a fuss of me.

Cassie seemed really pleased to have me back at school too. She kept coming over and talking to me, especially when I was with Hayley, like she was deliberately trying to get her mad. And then she actually invited me to hang out with her and Danielle at lunchtime. Hayley was furious.

But I still couldn't understand why the other girls disliked Cassie quite so much. I was beginning to think it was because they were all jealous. She certainly *was* the best looking girl in the class. And she was definitely the coolest and the bravest and, to be honest, the scariest.

Ruth told me Cassie's brother, Connor, was in year ten and really tough – no one messed with

him. So no one messed with Cassie. But I reckoned Cassie would've been pretty good at looking after herself anyway. She's got a really sharp tongue. Whatever anyone says to her, she always comes back with something better. Funnier. She even puts the boys down.

Although she pretends she isn't, Cassie's dead clever too but once, when I first met her, she told me, 'School's one big yawn. The smart thing is, to do the least you can to stay out of bother.'

Sometimes, though, a bit of bother's just what Cassie seems to love, especially when she's bored. Like the time she nearly set the Food Technology room on fire.

We were making savoury muffins. Cassie was working with Danielle and the two of them started this food fight – you know, flicking muffin mixture in each other's hair. Mrs Travis warned them a couple of times but Danielle wouldn't stop so she got sent to the Referral Room.

After that, Cassie wouldn't do anything she was told and, as soon as Mrs Travis turned her back, she put our recipe sheets in the ovens, while the muffins were still baking. There was a terrible smell of burning paper and one oven started pouring out black smoke. Mrs Travis said we were to leave the ovens closed and let the paper burn itself out but by then the room was full of smoke and smelled disgusting.

 87

It was so funny – I know it *could* have been dangerous, but it wasn't. Cassie ended up with a double detention and a real ear-wigging from the Head. She wasn't bothered about that, though. She told me afterwards, 'Detentions are no big deal. I can get a whole book read in an hour.' And everyone knows Cassie can write lines faster than anyone in the school.

I had no idea why Cassie seemed to have decided she wanted to hang out with me. I couldn't believe *she'd* have been taken in by all the makeover stuff. But over the next week or two I started to hang out with her whenever I got the chance. Apart from the fact we had some great laughs, it was only when I was with Cassie that I really stopped worrying about my mum – stopped feeling bad about not wanting to go home and be with her – stopped thinking about what a horrible person I was. When I was with Cassie it didn't matter what I said or did – it was OK. I felt more like Izzy again – braver and cooler – more fun.

As soon as I mentioned to Cassie on that Monday about wanting a mobile phone she said, 'No probs, Cutie,' which was what she'd started to call me. 'What colour d'ya fancy? How much d'ya wanna pay? I'll talk to my bro. It's sorted – leave it to me.'

fourteen

A few days later, Cassie came into school with this really neat, souped-up mobile, with a camera and a cute little animated screensaver and polyphonic ring tones. It had everything. She said, since I was her mate, her brother had said I could have it for twenty-five pounds.

I told Cassie I'd give her the money as soon as I could, but she said, 'It's cool, you can take the phone now. We know where you live,' she laughed. 'If you don't pay up, my brother'll send his mates round.'

She was only joking though, I'm sure.

When I got home I showed Chip my new phone and he was well-impressed. He said the ring tone was rubbish, but he offered to download something better from the Internet for me, so we went on his computer. We didn't hear Max coming in from school.

Suddenly, she was standing at Chip's bedroom door watching us.

'You two are getting very pally all of a sudden,' she said, but like she didn't approve of it. I

wondered for a minute if she was a bit jealous, but that just seemed silly. Chip ignored Max like he does most of the time, but I didn't want to make her mad again so I started to tell her how many people at school were beginning to copy my clothes and my hair. She half-smiled at that.

'They're not as good as mine, though,' I told her.

Max looked surprised. 'You're getting a bit full of yourself,' she said.

'It's true,' I said. 'They're not.' I meant it as a compliment; she was the one who'd chosen everything.

But Max shook her head. She spotted the phone. 'What you got there?'

So I showed her my new mobile. That was a mistake. When she found out I'd got it from Cassie McCloud's brother, she went off like a rocket.

'Are you a complete idiot? Haven't I told you to stay away from her? Don't you realise it's bound to have fallen off the back of a lorry?' I must have looked blank then, because she said, 'Oh, wake up, why don't you? *Nicked*. You know, *hot*? That's what her family's like. I warned you, didn't I?'

I told myself I didn't believe what Max was saying. Cassie would never get involved in stolen stuff. I knew Max didn't like Cassie, for some

reason. If Max wasn't so cool herself, I might have thought that she was a bit jealous of Cassie, too, and that was what this was all about.

'Look, you don't know it's stolen, Max,' Chip joined in. 'It might be genuine. Just give her a break, why don't you.'

Max glared at Chip, but then she walked off in a strop. Chip grinned, like we'd done something clever – managed to have the last word over Max for once. But I just felt like I'd got on her bad side – yet again.

Later, when Mum rang, I decided to tell her about my new phone. She still didn't know about the rest of the money and now, with the cancer, there was no way Auntie Paula was going to risk upsetting her more. But I thought it couldn't hurt to tell her about the mobile.

I said, 'Everyone else has got one, Mum. And it wasn't expensive. And I used my own money…'

But she cut in, 'It's OK, Bella. You don't have to convince me. It is your money, I suppose. Seems a silly waste, but what do I know? If you must have what everyone else has…'

I couldn't believe it, but Mum did seem to be getting a bit more laid back. Or maybe she was just too tired to want to argue with me. It was still quite hard finding safe things to talk to her about. To be honest, I hated hearing how sick and tired

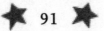

the chemotherapy made her, and she didn't seem to want to talk about it either.

But whenever Mum asked me about school and I tried to tell her about Hayley or some of the other girls in my class, she didn't seem interested. All she wanted to know was what we were doing in lessons and whether I was getting good grades and if I was keeping out of trouble, which wasn't so hard at first – like I said, I'd always been good at that. But as I was starting to get more friendly with Cassie McCloud, suddenly it wasn't quite so easy.

Danielle's family come from Jamaica and when they went back there for a six-week trip, Cassie wanted me to sit with her in class every day. After that neither of us got much work done. We had a lot of laughs, though, which is how I got my first detention.

It was over my mobile phone. I know everyone else has had a phone like *for ever*, but I honestly don't know how I lived without mine up till then. Suddenly, it was the first thing I checked in the morning and the last thing I looked at before I went to sleep at night.

At first Hayley sent me text messages all the time, about homework, things she'd seen on TV, to remind me I was going to tea the next day, anything really. Then I started getting all these other texts as well, with no name on them. You

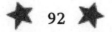

could tell they were from boys! I didn't need two guesses who this one came from:

ROSES R RED, VIOLETS R BLUE

TIL U MAKE UP UR MIND WE BOTH LOVE U.

I don't know who gave them my number because I certainly didn't. I found this message at the beginning of French with Mr Hathaway. I was showing it to Cassie under my desk, trying to be quiet about it.

Cassie had warned me when I first got the phone to be careful who I gave my number to. She thinks most people in our class are a waste of space, especially the boys. So when she saw the message she wrinkled up her forehead and mouthed, 'Who's that from?'

When I nodded at Betty and Doris she just about fell off her chair. I'd never told Cassie about them stalking me.

'Those two donkeys?' she snorted and let out this really loud laugh. The whole class started up then and Mr Hathaway had a lot of trouble quietening everyone down. So he confiscated my phone – which you're not supposed to have in school, but everybody does – for the rest of the day and sent us both to spend the lunch hour in the Referral Room.

All morning I couldn't help worrying about it. I thought detentions were bound to be a bit scary, but I'd worried for nothing, this one wasn't. There

were only the two of us, and two boys from year nine who'd been scrapping on the way to school. They played cards while Cassie and me read the romantic bits out of her Mills and Boon to each other. Miss Holden, the teacher on duty, was trying to get her marking done and, apart from telling us now and again to keep the noise down, she didn't seem to care.

I was relieved. Cassie was right; it was no big deal.

When I got home that night, Chip started teasing me about turning into a delinquent. I told him, 'I blame those two idiots for sending the message in the first place. I'll brain whoever it was gave them my number.'

Chip went really pink, right to his ears. I couldn't believe it.

'You rat!' I said. 'What did you do that for?'

'They paid me two quid,' he said. '*Each*! That's well over the going rate.'

'What does that mean?' I asked.

But Chip just shrugged and grinned.

'Anyway,' he said, 'what's the problem? They're about as dangerous as a pair of hamsters.' Max was right about Chip; he'll do just about anything for money.

I'd been thinking it was lucky I'd got the detention in school time; I didn't want Auntie Paula to find out. But I should have known who would find out. I don't know how she had so quickly, though.

Max came home, all guns blazing.

'Maybe you'll believe me now,' she said, throwing her bag on the floor. 'Now she's got you in real trouble.'

'It's only a detention,' I said, just like Cassie would. 'I don't know what all the fuss is about.'

But then Max really flipped.

'Don't think people haven't noticed how you're changing,' she yelled. 'You might think you're Miss Popularity, but you want to be very careful, all that could change too, you know!'

'I'm glad I'm changing,' I said right back. 'And I like being popular, why wouldn't I?'

But that just made Max more exasperated with me. 'For goodness sake, Izzy. This isn't just about hair and stuff. People need to like you for more than just your hair, some already do. It's who you truly are that matters.' Then she stormed off.

fifteen

The next weekend it was Amber's birthday sleepover. Since I'd been sitting with Cassie in class all the other girls had been a bit cool with me, so I was relieved that Amber had still invited me. I was really looking forward to it. I'd slept once or twice at Dawn's house, but that's not like a proper sleepover party. There were going to be nine of us including Amber: Hayley, Jacquette, Ruth, Lauren, Beccy, Naomi, me, and Amber's cousin, Jade.

Cassie wasn't invited, obviously, so I couldn't say much about it in front of her. She didn't care, though; she'd already told me she thought Hayley and her friends were pretty silly. She called them the Tweenies.

'Have fun at your pyjama party,' Cassie said sarcastically to me at the end of school on Friday. 'Don't get too excited.'

But I was excited; I could hardly wait. I couldn't imagine where we'd all sleep. You'd never have fitted nine people in my bedroom at home. But Amber's mum and dad pushed the furniture back

and let us all sleep in the lounge on the floor. After we'd watched a video and her parents had gone off to bed we sat up eating sweets and chocolate even though only a couple of hours earlier we'd had a big barbecue supper.

Amber had asked me to bring all the things for *Zig-Zagging* so I could show everyone how to do their hair like mine. While we were doing hair and make-up and things, Amber said we had to tell each other our deepest secrets, like which boys we fancied, what was the most embarrassing thing that'd ever happened to us, that kind of thing. I didn't tell them anything much, even though they kept on at me. I certainly wasn't going to tell anyone about fancying Damian.

It was going great, until they started talking about people from school. Soon they were being horrible about Cassie and Danielle, but especially Cassie.

Hayley started it: 'Both her brothers are in and out of trouble with the police, you know.'

'They're a really rough family,' Amber agreed.

'When Ruth's dinner money disappeared it was her that took it,' said Jacquette. 'Definitely.'

'We don't know that,' Ruth said. 'Not for sure.'

Hayley and Amber rolled their eyes. I couldn't say anything, it had happened before I was in the class, but they all seemed to think that by not joining in, I was defending Cassie.

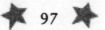 97

'Izzy seems to get on very well with her,' said Jacquette.

I shrugged. 'She seems OK to me,' I said.

'That's because you don't know her yet,' said Amber.

'She's only being nice to you to get at me,' said Hayley.

I must have looked as if I didn't really get what she was saying, because Jacquette said, quite sharply, 'It's like when Hayley and Danielle were best friends. She wasn't happy 'till she'd split them up.'

'We're just warning you what she's like,' added Beccy.

'And we know your Maxine doesn't like you being friends with her,' Hayley said. And suddenly I knew how Max had found out about my detention and about me spending time with Cassie.

They were all watching me now. I was so sick of people telling me what to do – Mum, Max, now them. I really wanted to tell them to mind their own business. But I still wasn't brave enough. I felt like Bella again, on the outside of the group, all knotted up and scared inside. Too much of a coward to say what I thought. When I was with Cassie I didn't feel like that. She didn't belong to any kind of group either, but that didn't seem to bother her. She was brave enough on her own. I suppose I was hoping that some of her bravery might rub off on me.

I was glad when they finally turned out the lights. I lay listening to them telling rude jokes and thought, Cassie's right, they are just silly kids.

When I got home and Max asked me if I'd enjoyed the party I didn't say any of that to her, though. I said it had been OK.

'Just OK? Well, come on,' she said. 'Let's hear all about it.'

But I only told her about the video and the food and the *Zig-Zagging*. I didn't give her *all the grisly details.* I thought, if she really wants to know, she's only got to go and ask her spies.

When Auntie Paula got back later that day from visiting Mum, she brought me a nice long letter and a couple of presents. Although she'd been going up every weekend, I hadn't been home again since that first time. Mum had said she didn't really want me to go while she was being so sick all the time, and now that her hair was falling out with the chemotherapy. I could hardly bear to think about that. But at least Auntie Paula said Mum had seemed in better spirits.

I opened my presents: a couple of pairs of knickers, a T-shirt and some magazines. I knew Auntie Paula must have bought the T-shirt, it was far trendier than Mum would have chosen.

'It's not your birthday, is it?' Max asked.

'No,' said Auntie Paula. 'It's just a couple of little things from her mum 'cos she's missing her.

Your birthday's near the end of June, isn't it, sweetheart? With a bit of luck you'll be home in time for that.'

Later, when we were on our own, Max said, 'I'd have thought it ought to be the other way round – you sending your mum presents, since she's the one who's ill. Although I suppose you've got no money left for presents now you've spent it all on mobile phones and things!'

For a moment, I was really annoyed with Max. For a start it wasn't true that I had no money left to spend on my mum. I just hadn't thought about sending her a present. And anyway, spending most of my money had been Max's idea in the first place.

Suddenly, I heard myself saying to her, 'In case you've forgotten, you were the one who said it's *my* money and I should be able to do exactly what I want with it!'

I could see Max was shocked. It was the first time I'd really answered her back and she didn't look happy about it.

She snatched her magazine off the bed and went stomping downstairs. My face felt really hot and, for a few minutes, my stomach was all churned up. I think I expected her to come storming back, but she didn't. I couldn't believe I'd done it. But I thought, well, I'm right, aren't I? And if Max doesn't like it, too bad.

I took the magazines Mum had sent me and

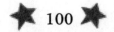 100

started to read them, lying on my bed – not as cool as an ice-cube, exactly, but cool as a cucumber, maybe.

But after a few minutes lying there, I had to admit, to myself at least, that of course I *did* feel guilty about my mum a lot of the time – about not being there to help her. I was here, having fun with my friends, while she was ill, on her own at home. Sometimes even thinking about Mum made it hurt when I tried to breathe. But there wasn't anything I could do about it. That's why I kept pushing it to the back of my mind. Max didn't understand – it wasn't her mum had cancer, though, was it?

And there wasn't really anyone else I could talk to about it either. Not even Cassie. And any chance I might have had to talk to Max, to make her understand, I'd blown completely. I'd never had so many friends before in my life, and yet there wasn't one of them I could talk to like I used to be able to talk to Dawn. It was the first time I realised how much I was really missing her.

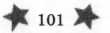

sixteen

After I got over the shock of standing up to Max and actually surviving it, I realised how good it was to say what I felt for a change. Not to be scared and bottled up all the time, like Bella. After all, wasn't that what Max had been trying to get me to do – to stand up for myself? So it gave me the nerve to try it again.

I'd been getting more brainless messages from Betty and Doris. I knew that I should have told them by now to leave me alone, that I wasn't interested in either of them, but I still hadn't known how to do it without hurting their feelings. Suddenly, I didn't care about that.

The next day, when I was walking into school, I saw them in the corridor. I marched straight up to them. 'Listen you pair – just stop sending me silly messages. If you've got something to say to me you can say it to my face instead of hiding behind your mobile phones. You're being pathetic.'

They looked really surprised and to tell you the truth – so was I.

But even after Betty and Doris stopped texting

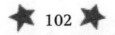 102

me I carried on getting other anonymous texts. I had no idea how many people Chip had sold my number to *at the going rate* and I'd given up asking him! Mostly the messages were plain stupid, so obviously they came from boys. But one or two were quite nice and said things like:

NICE OUTFIT 2DAY.

or

THAT TOP MATCHES UR EYES.

When I showed Cassie, she groaned. 'How sad is that?'

I didn't think it was sad. I secretly hoped the messages might have come from Damian, but I knew that was probably another silly fairy tale idea of mine. Then something happened at school – just something small – but enough to start me off hoping again. One day I'd been sitting out on the field at lunchtime with Cassie. I was spending even less time with Hayley and the others since the sleepover. I must have left my jacket on the grass, I hadn't missed it yet. But when afternoon school started and Damian and his friends came into the classroom he was carrying it over his shoulder. He dropped it on my desk and said, 'I think this might be yours, Funky Boots.'

Then Damian grinned at me. That was all there was to it, but I got all hot and bothered anyway. And I couldn't help myself, as soon as he was out

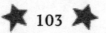

of earshot I almost squealed, '*Funky Boots?!*'

'It's no big deal,' Cassie said in a bored voice. Then she looked at me suspiciously. 'Unless you've got a crush on him.'

Even though she was my friend, I didn't want Cassie to know. I wasn't sure why not. It was the one little secret I wanted to keep to myself. So I shook my head and tried to pretend I didn't know what she was on about. But I couldn't bring myself to actually lie about it. 'He's OK, I suppose,' I shrugged.

Cassie was still looking straight at me, but then she just wrinkled her nose. 'Le Blanc?' she said, glancing over at him. 'Naaa, too pretty. Not my type at all.' And then, luckily, she let the subject drop.

At home, Max had called a kind of truce, partly because she'd lost interest in me and found a new project.

I was still talking to Mum on the phone every night, but now after each call Max wanted *all the grisly details*. If she wasn't satisfied with the answers I gave her she'd get on the phone herself and talk to my mum, sometimes for far longer than I did, which I didn't feel too happy about.

Max had been doing some sewing. When it was finished, she let me see it. It was a beautiful scarf with sequins and bits of gold running through it.

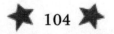

'It's *gorgeous*,' I said. 'Who's it for?'

She looked at me a bit surprised. 'Your mum, of course.'

'*My* mum?' I said, equally surprised.

Max shook her head, as if I was completely beyond hope. 'She's losing her *hair*. You know…' she said it as if she was talking to a toddler, 'with the chemotherapy?' I felt like using her favourite expression: tell me something I don't know, Max. But of course I didn't.

She said, 'Honestly, Izzy, I don't know what goes on in your head.'

I just looked away, I wasn't going to admit it to her, but to be honest, sometimes I didn't really know myself. Still, part of me wished I'd come up with the scarf idea. Max was good at that kind of thing – like my makeover – making things fun, even something as horrible as my mum losing her hair. Why couldn't I be like that?

And now Max told me, she was planning a makeover for Auntie Paula and Uncle Dougie. After what had happened to my mum, she'd decided they needed a lifestyle makeover. And since they weren't doing it themselves, she'd have to do it for them.

Instead of reading her fashion magazines, Max started buying things like *HealthyLiving* and *Fit and Fabulous*. I'd find them lying open on articles about 'How to stay fit and live a long and healthy

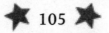

life.' She asked me lots of questions too, like – had Mum ever been a smoker? Did she drink alcohol regularly? Had she ever taken drugs?

Drugs! Honestly, you could tell Max didn't have a clue about my mum.

She wanted to know, did she take any exercise? Was she overweight? Max said, according to the charts in one magazine, both Auntie Paula and Uncle Dougie were almost 'clinically obese', which I thought showed what rubbish she was reading. To be honest, I was soon sick of the subject. It made me think about lots of things I was trying hard *not* to think about.

I started to feel sorry for Auntie Paula when Max got on her case. Auntie Paula's a little bit plump, I suppose, more than my mum anyway, but it's not like she spends a lot of time sitting on her bottom. She's always on the go. But Max told her that wasn't the same as aerobic exercise and she ought to join a gym. Auntie Paula burst out laughing. Then Max started asking her if she'd ever had her cholesterol tested, whether she did regular breast examinations and when her last smear test had been.

'OK,' Auntie Paula said, '*that's it!*' She told Max she'd gone quite far enough and she could safely leave her to look after her own bits and pieces, thank you very much.

So Max moved on to Uncle Dougie, who she

said was more of a sitting target. As she reminded him, he spent all day, every day, being driven round in a car and on top of that he was a smoker.

'Hardly a smoker,' Uncle Dougie insisted. 'I only have seven cigarettes a day, and never in the house.'

But Max said, 'That's seven too many and you've gotta give up.'

Over breakfast Max read him all the statistics about smoking-related illnesses and at night she made him watch the terrible ads they have on TV.

In the end Uncle Dougie said, 'OK, OK, I give in.' He said giving up smoking couldn't be any harder than being hounded by Max day in, day out.

The only person Max didn't get on to was Chip. It wasn't that she didn't try, it was just that it made no impression on him. It was like he was completely deaf to her. I wondered whether, if I'd lived all my life with Max, I'd have been able to ignore her too.

On the phone, when Mum was going on at me about whether I was doing my homework, and helping Auntie Paula with the dishes and stuff (which I wasn't so often now, but only because I'd been so busy) and keeping up with my flute practice (which I wasn't at all because – yawn, yawn – I was trying to forget I even played it!) once or twice perhaps I snapped at Mum a bit. But Max always seemed to hear me if I did. Then

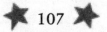

she'd give me this big talking to about speaking to my mum more sensitively – when Mum had such a lot to deal with. And if I just thought about her a bit more...

I already knew all that. But like I said before, I didn't want to think about it. How would it help Mum me worrying anyway? Hadn't Max said I'd always done far too much worrying? Well, Izzy didn't intend to. Sometimes, at school, when I was with Cassie, I managed to forget about it all for hours on end and have a bit of fun. But at home, Max was always there to remind me again.

Honestly, talk about nag, nag, nag. It was like Max had turned from being my scary fairy godmother into my boring fairy godmother. Well, I didn't need Max's opinions and advice any more and I was getting close to telling her so.

seventeen

The following weekend was going to be half-term. I could hardly believe how quickly it had come round. Mum must have been feeling a bit less sick because she asked Auntie Paula to bring me with her for a visit. When we talked on the phone, she started making jokes – about how she looked like a bald eagle; how I'd never recognise her now she was an egg-head. But my mum doesn't really do jokes and none of these were funny.

Auntie Paula tried to make it sound like it was no big deal too. She said Mum's hair would soon grow back, but in the meantime she'd probably need a wig. In fact, she'd got a couple from her hairdresser for Mum to try on.

'We can all try them,' she said. 'Have a little wig party. It'll be fun.'

Fun?! It didn't sound like fun to me. It sounded absolutely horrible. I didn't want to see my mum without any hair. Or wearing some stupid wig.

One time when Max wasn't around, I picked up the photo of Mum by my bed. I tried to cover up all her hair with my fingers, trying to imagine her

completely bald. I just couldn't. I thought she wouldn't look like my mum any more. I was scared I wasn't going to recognise her. It was already weeks since I'd seen her.

At the beginning of her treatment, Mum often sounded too tired to talk on the phone – like this really old person. But now she'd started feeling a bit better, she'd turned into this other person who talked nonstop, making pathetic jokes! But neither of them sounded like my mum.

I knew that I'd changed, but I didn't want her to.

At school things weren't going so well either. Betty and Doris were still pestering me, and now Hayley joined in on their side.

'I think you're being mean, keeping them both dangling on a string,' she said.

I couldn't see what it had to do with her. Anyway, I told her, I wasn't keeping anyone on a string. I said, 'It's not my fault if they want to follow me about like a pair of puppies. Like Cassie says, it's a free country.'

I knew Hayley wouldn't like that, but then things between Hayley and me were coming to a head anyway.

Over half-term, Jacquette was having a sleepover and this time I wasn't invited. I didn't say anything, because I was beginning to think I couldn't have cared less, but when we were

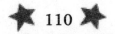

on our own Hayley said, 'We tried to warn you, Izzy. I'm afraid you're just going to have to choose. It's her – or us.'

This time I didn't bottle out. I wasn't going to be told what to do. I didn't turn back into mousy Bella. Izzy was ready to stand up to her.

'I couldn't care less about your silly sleepover,' I told Hayley.

I said I was bored with hanging out with them, and having them copy everything I did, and everything I wore, as if they didn't have minds of their own. If I hadn't been going away at half-term anyway, I said, I'd far rather have met Cassie and gone into town with her, which was bound to be a much better laugh.

Hayley went bright pink. She said that was fine by them because I obviously wasn't the kind of person they wanted to hang out with any more.

'You certainly had us fooled in the beginning,' she said. 'I suppose we should have known what to expect, though, given your reputation. Cassie McCloud's welcome to you. You're two of a kind.'

I didn't say anything back. It wasn't worth it. It had been great being friends with Hayley in the beginning, but I felt as if I'd grown out of her and her friends. Now I'd far rather hang out with Cassie. She was right when she said I was way too cool – and wild like her – to go around with the Tweenies.

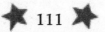

That evening, it was clear Max's spies had been at work again. She came into the bedroom when I was trying to decide what clothes to pack for the weekend at Mum's.

'I hope you realise everyone's talking about you,' she said, quite spitefully.

I said, '*Everyone*? Oh, good.'

Max looked daggers at me.

'That was the idea, wasn't it, to stand out from the crowd? To be noticed? To be your own person? Isn't that what you told me?'

That shut Max up for once. What *could* she say? She just shook her head, as if there was no hope for me.

After she'd left the room I found myself shaking my head too because, although I'd got the last word, I hadn't wanted to fall out with Max again. I hated it when there was an atmosphere in the bedroom.

Later on, I tried to smooth things over by asking her what she thought about an outfit I was thinking of taking with me to Mum's. She almost snapped my head off. 'There are more important things than clothes you know, *Izzy*. Your mum could be dying, for goodness sake!'

I just froze. Max gasped and went red in the face. 'I'm sorry, Izzy. I'm sorry, I didn't mean to say that. I wasn't…I didn't…just forget it. OK?'

But I couldn't say anything. Max went

downstairs again, leaving me sitting on my bed, stunned. You'll probably think: how dumb are you but, until then, I honestly hadn't thought my mum's illness was as serious as that. I knew she had cancer, but Auntie Paula had said she'd get better – and she was doing that at the moment. I'd never thought…I'd never *let* myself think…my mum could die!

I was so angry with Max. Who did she think she was, saying something like that? My mum was *not* going to die. Max liked to think she knew *everything*, but Auntie Paula was a midwife, she knew about medical things, she'd told me Mum was getting better every day.

I stuffed everything into my case. Suddenly, I couldn't wait to get home. I wanted to be at least two hundred miles away from Max. I didn't care what Mum said, I wasn't coming back here. Ever.

I got undressed and into bed and lay there in the dark, trying hard not to think about anything. Soon I'll be asleep, I told myself, and then I won't be able to think. But I couldn't get to sleep. I felt like I'd swallowed a massive stone that was stuck halfway down my throat.

A little while later, I heard the bedroom door open and Auntie Paula whispered my name, 'Izzy, are you OK? Has Max been upsetting you?'

I stayed absolutely still and pretended to be asleep, until she went away.

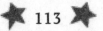 113

Max came upstairs about half an hour later. Again, I pretended I was asleep, but Max wasn't so easy to fool. She kept whispering, 'Izzy? Izzy, are you awake? Can I come and talk to you?'

I was determined I wasn't going to talk to *her* – about anything. I kept on holding my breath, but she wouldn't leave me alone.

Suddenly, I felt her weight on the end of my bed. Then, through the quilt I could feel her hand on my leg.

'I really didn't mean it, Izzy,' she started to say. 'Izzy, please, listen…'

But I pushed her hand away and hissed at her, *'Don't, Max! Just don't!'*

eighteen

Auntie Paula didn't say anything about the night before. And we'd left Manchester early, before Max was awake. For the first hour we didn't talk much. Auntie Paula put the radio on and I just watched the miles go by. We stopped halfway at a service station and I bought some flowers for Mum.

'That's a really sweet thought,' Auntie Paula told me, which made me feel terrible because, I realised, it was the kind of thing I used to do all the time, but nowadays I wouldn't have thought about it if it hadn't been for Max the other day.

Auntie Paula was much more chatty after she'd had her coffee-fix. 'But don't tell Max,' she said. 'Apparently coffee's bad for you too.'

The journey was so different to that first one when Uncle Dougie had picked me up and I'd been little mousey-me, afraid to speak to him. Auntie Paula told me more stories about her and Mum, and their arguments. She didn't mention the fact that Max and I had fallen out, but I knew she was trying to remind me that when you had to

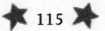

share a bedroom, even sisters argued. Max and I weren't sisters, but it *had* been feeling like that lately and it made me realise that when sisters didn't even like each other, it was worse than having no sister at all.

Auntie Paula was telling me this funny story about when she was a student mid-wife living in a flat in London. 'And I came home one night and the flat was empty,' she said. 'Nothing in it, *at all*. I thought I'd come into someone else's flat by mistake, but I hadn't. Everything I owned in the world, which wasn't much, believe me, had been nicked. Even my toothbrush. Even my dirty laundry! When I realised that I sat on the bare floorboards and started to laugh and I just couldn't stop.'

She said she'd rung my mum to tell her and Mum had been more upset than her. She'd shouted down the phone, 'Why can't you ever take anything seriously, Paula? Why is everything such a joke to you?'

That seemed to me to be the biggest difference between Auntie Paula and Mum – that Mum smiled sometimes, but she didn't often laugh, whereas Auntie Paula laughed so easily, even at Uncle Dougie's bad jokes. I couldn't imagine how they'd grown up in the same family.

It made me wonder what I'd have been like if I'd grown up in Auntie Paula's family instead of my

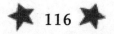

own? Or in my family but with a dad as well, who told bad jokes like Uncle Dougie. Would I still have been boring and quiet and shy – or different, better, more normal, even cooler, like Max?

We were getting closer to home and I was starting to feel nervous again. I must have gone quiet because Auntie Paula suddenly reached across and squeezed my arm. 'Oh, Izzy,' she said. 'Max was right, you know, that makeover was good for you. You look absolutely beautiful. Your mum's going to be so surprised when she realises how much you've grown up.'

I had hardly cried at all through everything that had happened, even over the last few days when I'd felt really mixed up and angry all the time, but suddenly I couldn't stop the tears. Auntie Paula just handed me a packet of tissues. That was another way she was different to my mum. Mum would have tried to stop me crying, or blamed herself for starting me off, and that would have made me feel worse. Just for one moment, even though it makes me feel horrible to admit it, I found myself wishing Auntie Paula was my mum.

When we got to my house it felt as if I hadn't seen it for years, instead of weeks. It seemed so much smaller for a start. Mum was looking out of the window for us. The front door opened before we'd even parked the car. If the house was smaller

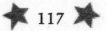

than I remembered, so was Mum. She looked as if she'd actually shrunk. And she was so thin! She had a scarf round her head that made her look like a funny old lady. Not like my mum at all.

Suddenly, she was hugging me and crying. When I tried to give her the flowers she cried all over again. It was awful. But Auntie Paula gave us both a hug and made a few jokes about getting the mop and bucket out before Mum flooded the place, then she steered us into the house.

At first it felt weird being back home, though it was good to be with Mum. I was thinking how different she looked and I'd forgotten how different I must seem to her. 'Just look at you!' she said. 'You're not my little Bella any more. Look at those clothes, as well as your hair!'

Before Mum could say too much more, Auntie Paula quickly changed the subject by offering to make us all a cup of tea.

'And I've brought some carrot cake,' she said. 'Your favourite, Lynda.'

Mum told me her appetite was improving, slowly, but she was still sleeping a lot. 'As soon as I start to get my energy back,' she said, 'you'll be able to come home. Perhaps in a few weeks, when I've finished the chemotherapy.'

A few weeks! I couldn't wait that long. I didn't want to go back to Manchester at all, not now everything was so horrible with Max. 'But I want

 118

to stay here,' I told Mum, 'and look after you. I've missed you. I hate that I can't do anything to help you get better.'

'Don't you think chatting to you on the phone every night helps, and seeing you – that's better than any medicine in the world?' she said, giving me a hug. 'Anyway you can see: I *am* getting better. And I thought you were enjoying being with your cousins. I thought you liked your new school.'

I couldn't tell Mum that all that was changing, not in front of Auntie Paula.

After lunch, Auntie Paula sent Mum for a lie-down.

Mum smiled at me, 'She's so bossy. Just because she's the oldest. You want to thank your lucky stars you haven't got a sister to boss you about.'

I could tell Mum was joking. I could see that with all the weekends they'd spent together, Mum and Auntie Paula were like a pair of old friends as well as sisters. I felt a bit jealous. It had been more like that with me and Max for a little while, until I messed it up.

I watched Mum go upstairs, stopping to catch her breath. Auntie Paula gave me a hug and said, 'Don't worry. She's getting better all the time. Now let's you and me get the work done, while your mum has a nap. You dust, I'll hoover. Then later we're going to have a lovely girlie time, just the three of us. No men or boys, what bliss!'

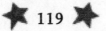 119

It was OK doing the housework – I hadn't been helping so much lately. I suppose my head had been full of other things. And anyway Chip never helped, and Max didn't do much around the house either. I supposed housework was just not very cool.

While I did the dusting I noticed lots of get-well cards that people from work had sent Mum. Auntie Paula said that lots of them had been to visit Mum too. We'd never had many visitors before – and never anyone from Mum's work.

Later, Auntie Paula made this really special supper, with my flowers on the table, and opened a bottle of wine. My mum never used to drink wine but she and Auntie Paula drank the whole bottle between them.

Max had sent the scarf she'd made, wrapped up in a lovely gift bag. It nearly made my mum cry when she saw it. She put it straight on, over the top of the scarf she was wearing – which looked a bit funny.

Auntie Paula suggested I take a photo with my mobile and send it to Max. Mum was surprised to see how tiny my phone was. She was really interested. I thought she'd start up again about what a waste of money it was, but she didn't.

In the photo, even though she looked a bit funny, Mum was smiling like she was really, really

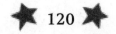

happy. I don't know if it was the wine that made her seem more laid back than usual, because she did keep giggling, but whatever it was I was glad about it. Smiling suited my mum far better than crying.

nineteen

After we'd eaten, I left Mum and Auntie Paula still sitting at the table, talking, and went up to my bedroom. When I first walked through the door I hardly recognised it. Compared to Max's bedroom, it looked like a little kid's.

I sat on my bed and checked my phone messages. There were two from Cassie:

HOWZIT GOIN? MISS YA. CALL ME IF U CAN.

And then:

WHEN U COMIN BACK?

I didn't know how I was going to tell Cassie that I wasn't coming back, that I was staying here with Mum. I hadn't told anyone at school about my mum having cancer. When people had asked me why I was living at Max's I'd just said Mum had had to go away for a while. I'd let them think it was for work, like she had this job that meant she needed to travel, which was so much cooler than them knowing that she was ill. It was just another lie I'd found myself telling because it seemed easier, I suppose.

I lay on my bed looking round my room. It

definitely needed one of Max's makeovers. It was full of rubbish – things I'd had since I was a baby. Why had I kept that stuff? It all reminded me of the old mousy-me. This was Bella's room; Izzy didn't fit in here. The first thing I was going to do, as soon as Mum was better, was have a complete clear-out. Persuade her to let me have bunks. Then, maybe in the summer holidays, Cassie could come to stay for a weekend.

My phone beeped to say a photo-message had come in. It was of Max, wearing a pair of silly rabbit's ears and holding a big message saying *Get Better Soon, Auntie Lynda.* I still felt cross with her but I knew I ought to go and show it to Mum.

When I went downstairs, I heard shrieks of laughter coming from the lounge. I couldn't believe my eyes when I opened the door. The room looked completely different. There were candles burning everywhere and Mum was sitting in front of a mirror while Auntie Paula did her make-up. They were both wearing wigs: Mum had on a long, dark wig and a pair of dangly earrings and Auntie Paula wore a short, red curly wig. They were drinking another bottle of wine.

Auntie Paula stood back to give me a better view. 'So, what do you think?'

Mum was giggling again. I probably looked a bit shocked, but mostly I felt jealous. Doing makeovers was our thing, mine and Max's.

Auntie Paula laughed. 'You needn't look like that,' she said, as if she'd read my mind. 'It's not just you young ones who can have makeovers, you know.'

'So…what do you think?' Mum asked again, tossing her head so the long wig swished around her shoulders.

I thought she looked stupid, but I couldn't tell her that. OK, it was better than that old lady-type scarf, but she still didn't look a bit like my mum.

'I dunno,' I said and shrugged.

'Well, perhaps Izzy's right,' said Auntie Paula. 'Let's try the other one.'

She whipped her own wig off, and swapped them round. Then they both looked into the mirror and burst out laughing.

'Now what do you think?' Auntie Paula asked me.

But I couldn't manage to say anything, I was too stunned. When they'd swapped the wigs around, just for a second I'd caught a glimpse of Mum's nearly bald head. It was white and shiny as an egg, with just a few tufts of hair left still growing. Seeing it made me feel scared and a bit sick.

'Cinderella and her ugly older sister,' Auntie Paula said. But she wasn't smiling any more. She gave my mum's shoulder a squeeze. Mum looked serious for a minute too, but then she took hold of a piece of the long wig and held it under her nose. She twiddled the end like a moustache.

'No – her 'andsome prince?' she said in a silly French accent and they both started laughing again.

I stood there thinking, this isn't right. My mum doesn't do jokes. And she doesn't do accents. I wanted to shout at them both, the way Mum had shouted at Auntie Paula: *my mum's got no hair. This isn't funny! Why are you both trying to make a joke out of it?*

They looked at me, waiting for me to join in, but when I didn't they stopped laughing too.

'You know who we need here to help us decide?' Mum said. 'Maxine.'

'Oh, yes, she's the Style Queen all right,' said Auntie Paula, taking off her own wig and perching it on my head. 'Which do you think Max would choose?'

'I don't know,' I said, irritably, knocking the wig on the floor. 'Why don't you ask her?' and I held out the phone to show them Max's photo message.

My mum's eyes filled up. 'What a sweet girl. I bet you're going to miss her when you come home, Bella.'

Suddenly, I wanted to scream at Mum, 'I'm not Bella any more. I'm Izzy!' Why couldn't she see that I knew about style, as well? I knew what was cool. She didn't need to ask Max.

But now I was home it felt like all that was disappearing – knowing what was cool and being

brave enough to say what I was thinking. I was starting to feel more like Bella again – nervous and curled up tight inside. In fact, it was being Izzy I couldn't remember properly any more.

I felt the tears stinging the back of my eyes and I wanted to get back to my bedroom before they started running down my face. I left Mum and Auntie Paula still laughing and swapping wigs.

I found a box at the back of my wardrobe and started chucking my old things into it. I wanted to smash them up. I tried to make myself, but Bella wasn't the kind of person who smashed things.

Long after I'd got into bed, I couldn't get to sleep. I kept on seeing Mum's head, so white and *bare.* Like seeing her with no clothes on. I lay awake, listening to her and Auntie Paula still laughing and playing their corny old music really loud. It was hard to believe but I think they were drunk.

I felt more on my own than ever. I didn't want to go back and have Max nagging me and spoiling my fun for the next few weeks. But I didn't want to stay at home and turn back into boring old Bella either. I could already feel myself sliding back into my old life and I didn't know how to stop that from happening.

Right then, I wasn't sure what I did want, but I knew I *didn't* want that!

126

twenty

Auntie Paula had completely cleared up by the time I came down next morning.

'I hope we didn't keep you awake last night,' she said. 'We were rather late and had more wine than was good for us. But your mum was looking so much better by the end of the evening, I think it was worth it.'

Auntie Paula suggested I take Mum a cup of tea in bed.

Mum was sitting up, wearing her scarf like a nightcap. 'You'd be surprised how cold your head gets at night, when there's no hair on it,' she joked.

I just wished she'd stop talking about it as if being bald was something ordinary. I changed the subject to something *I* wanted to talk about.

'Mum, do I *have* to go back with Auntie Paula?' I asked. 'I want to stay here with you. Please?'

Mum pulled me towards her and gave me a cuddle. 'Don't you think I want you home too? I can't wait. But I'm not ready to look after you yet.'

'I can look after myself!' I insisted.

'Oh, Bella, I know you think you've grown up while you've been away…'

'I have!' I insisted.

'Mmm,' said Mum, like she didn't really agree. 'In some ways, maybe. Look, it won't be for much longer, sweetheart, I promise.'

Then she told me how grateful I should feel to Auntie Paula – how very kind she'd been to Mum – how Mum would never have got through it without her. Mum's eyes started to fill up. I asked her how come there'd been all these years when they hadn't been friends, but Mum just shook her head and looked away.

'Oh, Bella, let's not talk about that,' she said.

And I was suddenly really mad again. Something else Bella wasn't allowed to ask about. But Izzy wanted to know. 'Why not?' I asked, a bit sharply. 'Why are there so many things we can't talk about?'

Mum looked shocked. 'What do you mean? What else can't we talk about?'

I couldn't believe she didn't know what I meant. I felt as if she ought to be able to read it on my forehead: *tell me about my dad, for a start!* But if it was there, Mum couldn't see it. 'It's not fair,' I almost shouted. 'You treat me like a baby. You never tell me anything.'

Mum looked even more shocked. Then her eyes really filled up and I started to feel horrible. I

knew Max had said that if something's important it's worth keeping after, but suddenly it didn't seem worth it to me, not if it was going to upset my mum that much. As Bella, I hated seeing Mum cry, so I gave her a hug and just left it alone. But afterwards I thought: what a coward, giving up that easily. I knew Max wouldn't have.

Later, Auntie Paula said she was taking Mum to do a little bit of shopping. She said some new clothes might cheer her up. I know it sounds stupid, but it was like they were copying me and Max again. So when Mum asked me if I wanted to go with them, I shook my head.

'Dawn's hoping to see you,' she reminded me, for the umpteenth time.

'Tell me something I don't know,' I snapped. 'I'm going. I'm going.'

Auntie Paula looked a bit surprised and so did Mum. 'It's just that she keeps on ringing,' she said, 'and I did promise her...'

I gave this big sigh, grabbed my jacket and left, banging the door behind me. I'd been trying to think of an excuse not to go to Dawn's, but I couldn't come up with one – even to myself.

On the way I saw one or two people from my old class. They didn't seem to recognise me and that suited me just fine. In my head I kept running through a few lame excuses why I hadn't rung or written. I wasn't sure Dawn would even speak to

me. I wouldn't have blamed her if she didn't.

When I got to Dawn's house I had to make myself go up the path and ring the doorbell. It felt like going to the dentist. But there was no one in. And then, instead of feeling relief, I was disappointed. Having got myself there I really did want to see Dawn. I wanted to be with a real friend again.

Suddenly a text message came through on my mobile. It was from Cassie:

HEY, CUTIE, MISSIN YA. CALL ME PRONTO.

And it was followed by a photo of Cassie with crossed eyes and her tongue sticking out. It really made me laugh. At least there was someone who could cheer me up if I had to go back to Manchester.

When Mum and Auntie Paula got back I told them Dawn wasn't in. I said I'd write or ring her the next week, but I knew I wouldn't. I'd worked out what had been putting me off going round in the first place: I didn't want to be Dawn's old friend, Ellie-bellie, the boring old mousy-me, any more. But I was pretty sure that the other me, the Izzy who hung around with girls like Cassie and Danielle, and fancied boys like Damian, wasn't the kind of person Dawn would want as a friend. No way.

When it was time to go back with Auntie Paula, I didn't even try to argue with Mum. When she said,

'It'll only be for a couple more weeks, maybe three at the most,' I just shrugged. By then I was glad I was going back. I knew I'd miss Mum much more, now that I'd been at home with her, but I was in no hurry to be boring old Bella again. Not yet.

I was really quiet in the car on the way home – Auntie Paula must have thought I was worrying about my mum, or not happy about going back with her to Manchester.

'You should tell me if there's anything we can do to make you feel more at home with us. How about asking Hayley or Amber to tea?' But I shook my head. There was no way either of them would want to come now. And I could see Max's face if I invited Cassie McCloud instead.

'Well, at least we should start planning your birthday,' Auntie Paula said, 'so you've got something to look forward to. Of course by then, you may well be home, but in case you're not. Have you ever been to Alton Towers? Max and Chip love going there. You could take a friend. What do you think?'

I couldn't believe it. I'd always wanted to go to Alton Towers but Mum would never have taken me. I couldn't wait to tell Cassie. OK, so Max wouldn't like it. But Auntie Paula had said I could take someone and Max could like it or lump it. It was *my* birthday.

When we got back, Max was out. Chip said

she'd dragged poor Uncle Dougie out on a bike ride down the canal tow-path. But later, when she came in, I was relieved to see she was at least trying to be a bit nicer to me, which made it easier.

When we were in bed, Max asked how Mum was doing, so I told her all about the makeover and the wigs. That really made her smile.

'Sounds like we've started a trend,' she said. And when I told her about her mum and my mum getting a bit drunk, she rolled her eyes and groaned. It was only when she asked about Dawn that things got a bit sticky again.

'I went round,' I said, 'but she wasn't in. I'm going to write to her this week.'

Max definitely looked as if she could tell I was lying. I sometimes felt with Max as if she could see inside my head and make sense of things I couldn't even make sense of myself.

It wasn't a very nice feeling, I can tell you.

twenty-one

The rest of half-term really dragged. Almost the minute I got back from Mum's, Cassie went off to Southport with her cousin and her auntie. I hardly saw anything of her. I was really bored and glad when school started back.

I wasn't looking forward to walking there on my own on Monday morning, though, so I was surprised, but relieved, when the doorbell rang as usual and Hayley, Lauren and Amber were standing outside.

'Are you ready?' they asked as if there had been no argument. I grabbed my things and went with them, but I felt uncomfortable and wondered why they'd changed their mind about me. I don't know if they were expecting me to be grateful, and grovel, but I didn't. I couldn't help noticing that even though they'd fallen out with me, they were still copying my clothes.

When we first got to school Cassie came straight over to talk to me. 'Got you a prezzie,' she said, waving a little glittery gift bag at me.

The others just made a ring round me and

stared at her, sort of freezing her out, but Cassie completely ignored them. She said, 'First period's PE. I'm bunking off, d'you wanna come?'

Hayley gave me a warning look, but when I didn't turn Cassie down straight off, she said, 'Don't think we're going to cover for you.'

'Did she ask you to?' Cassie said. Then she turned to me, 'Come on, it's easy, I've got a system. Let's lose these pathetic Tweenies!' and she walked away.

'Don't talk about us like that!' Hayley called after her. 'She's the pathetic one,' she said to me, expecting me to agree with her. But I knew whose side I was on, I didn't want Cassie thinking I wasn't cool any more. I started to follow her when Hayley pulled me back. 'We only gave you another chance,' she hissed, 'because Maxine asked us to. Because she told us – you know – about your mum and everything. But if you're going to do something stupid like this…'

I couldn't believe my ears. Max had asked them to give me another chance! Why on earth had she done that? And told them about my mum! She had no right. I was sick of her interfering in my life. I didn't need her to be my bossy fairy godmother any more. I'd got my cool clothes and hairstyle – and now I'd got my own friends too. If she didn't like them, well, tough, that was her problem.

'You don't have to worry about me any more,' I

told Hayley. 'I can take care of myself, thanks!'

Sad, boring old Bella might have put up with Max trying to organise the Tweenies to make sure I didn't have any fun, but Izzy certainly wasn't going to.

'She'll drop you when Danielle comes back,' Hayley warned me. 'She only wants to show she can take you off me.'

'Why would she want to do that?' I asked her.

'To prove she can,' said Hayley.

I thought what a load of rubbish that was. I was sure Hayley was just jealous. I knew this was absolutely my last chance with her and the others...but I couldn't have cared less. I shrugged and walked off, leaving them with their mouths open like a load of goldfish.

Unfortunately, Cassie's system didn't work. For once, Miss Howkins did a proper register...and we got a detention. That was the first of three I got in that same week. The second one was from Mr Baker – for breaking a couple of magnets in science. They fell on the floor and broke in half when we tried to see if they'd stick to the underwires in Cassie's bra. We really cracked up.

The third was the best laugh though.

It happened in Food Technology again. Cassie put a bar of soap in the microwave – just for a laugh. You've never seen anything like the mess it

made. It took a whole lunch hour for us to chip it off. But it was worth it. Everyone stood up and cheered when it exploded. Goodness knows why Mrs Travis made such a big deal out of it. It wasn't like it was dangerous or anything.

'Nice one, girls,' Damian said as he passed us in the corridor after we'd finished. And he high-fived with Cassie. I think he might have been meaning to do it with me, but I was scared I might get it wrong, so I quickly looked the other way. But I could feel myself blushing and I couldn't hide it.

'I *knew* it!' Cassie said. 'You really have got a crush.'

I tried to change the subject, but finally Cassie got it out of me. And this time I admitted how dishy I thought Damian was. I'd been so scared to tell her, but once I'd done it, I was glad. I even managed to seem quite cool about it and told Cassie I thought he just might have a little, *tiny* thing about me.

'You never know,' she said. 'Stranger things have happened. I could always find out if you like. I'll ask him.'

I had to beg her to promise she wouldn't and even then I couldn't be sure. Like I said, you never knew what Cassie might do.

The present Cassie had given me on the first day back at school was a pair of big gold hoop

earrings, like hers. She'd brought me them back from Southport. I was well chuffed, except that I'd never had my ears pierced, so I couldn't wear them. But Cassie said, 'No sweat, we'll go into town next weekend and get them done.'

It was the first time I'd been to the shops since I'd gone with Max and it was almost as exciting. Cassie showed me her fave places, which were different to the places I'd been with Max. And even trendier and cheaper. I was nervous about getting my ears done, but Cassie kept teasing me and so I had to pretend I was dead cool about it and suddenly it was done.

Auntie Paula was usually so laid back; I couldn't understand why she was bothered about it. 'If I'd realised what Max was starting all those weeks ago…' she began, but trailed off. 'I don't think your mum's going to like this one little bit, Izzy. I really wish you'd talked to me first.'

Of course it was too late by then, but that didn't stop Max piling on the nagging.

'What *do* you look like?' she said to me. 'I don't need three guesses whose idea this was.'

And she started making horrible remarks about *cloning* after Cassie showed me how to wear my hair tied back like hers too.

I was learning to smile and close my ears to Max, just like Chip did most of the time. But when

 137

she heard about the three detentions and started on at me about those, I just lost my rag.

'What's got into you?' she started. 'You'd think with your mum ill, you'd try and stay out of trouble, but you seem determined to go looking for it. I don't understand why you're behaving like a...a...'

'Wild child?' I finished off Max's sentence for her. 'Wasn't that part of your big makeover plan?' I asked her.

'I didn't mean you to turn into this,' Max yelled, waving a hand at me and pulling a disgusted face.

'So what did you mean?' I yelled back.

Max just groaned, as if I was too stupid to understand.

'You told me to learn to stand up for myself,' I reminded her, 'but you don't like it now when I do.'

'Fine! Whatever! But being horrible to people isn't cool, Izzy,' Max snapped back and stormed off.

I didn't need Max telling me I was changing, I knew that for myself. But changing was good, wasn't it? She'd obviously thought I needed to change or she wouldn't have done the makeover in the first place. I was having more fun than I'd ever had before. I didn't need a fairy godmother now, especially a bossy one. And the sooner Max realised that, the better.

Up 'till then, I'd been trying to keep the peace

at least. But when it looked like I would still be at the Ross's for my birthday and I finally asked Cassie to come to Alton Towers, I knew it would be like the final declaration of war as far as Max was concerned. Well, good! I thought.

Cassie was really over the moon when I asked her. I'd thought Alton Towers was somewhere she'd have been before but she said she hadn't. She acted as if I'd given *her* a birthday present. See, I told myself, Cassie's just like you, she hasn't had a lot of things that all the other kids have. Perhaps that was another reason I was attracted to her.

'Who else's going?' she asked me almost straightaway.

I didn't know. 'I suppose Chip'll take Fishy,' I said. 'I don't know if Max'll come.' I was hoping she wouldn't.

Cassie was quiet for a bit, as if she was thinking something through.

'Mmm,' she whispered, more to herself than to me. 'Perfect.'

I wondered if she might be planning a little birthday surprise for me.

A bit later she said, 'I've just had a great idea. Why don't you invite Damian to Alton Towers?'

I couldn't believe it, the way she came out with it like that. She caught me off guard and I went bright pink and shook my head.

'I'll ask him if you like,' she said, grinning.

I almost screamed at her, 'Don't you dare!'

'Are you daring me?' she said slowly. And her face suddenly changed. It went dead hard and serious. 'Because if you are…'

I was trying to tell if she meant it or not. Sometimes Cassie did scare me a bit, even now. I could still never be quite sure what she was going to do next.

Suddenly she burst out laughing. 'You should see your face,' she said, grinning again. 'You look scared to death. Can't you take a joke?'

I tried to smile, let her think I'd known she was fooling all the time, but for a second I'd thought: what if Max was right about Cassie? What if she was a bit of a dangerous person to hang out with? But I pushed that thought away just as quickly. It was too late to think about that now, anyway, there wasn't really anyone else left.

Besides, like Cassie said, we made a great pair. We were the coolest, funniest, grooviest, wildest girls in our year. Cassie and Izzy really rock, she told me. Oh, yes!

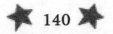

twenty-two

The next couple of weeks, all I could seem to think about was my birthday. If ever I did get a bit down about Mum, Cassie would make me laugh or tease me about Damian or remind me about Alton Towers and I'd be up again.

Even when Hayley and Amber and the other girls were giving me horrible looks and I started to feel as if everyone hated me, Cassie said, 'Only the toddler group. And who needs them.'

But it wasn't only the girls who'd gone off me. Finally Betty and Doris had given up. Cassie had made sure of that.

'What game are you playing with those two wombles?' she'd asked me one day.

I'd said it wasn't a game, that they were just harmless idiots really. I suppose it was a bit pathetic, the way they still came over at breaktimes, offering to share their snacks with me, but when Cassie told them to get lost and stop littering the place up I felt really bad. 'That wasn't very nice,' I said.

'Look, Izzy, if you're hanging out with me,

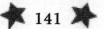 141

you don't hang around with wombles, OK? Your choice.'

I could see she meant it. I just shrugged and smiled at her. What else could I do? Besides, if I had to make a choice, it was always going to be someone cool like Cassie. Obviously. And if it hadn't been for her I'd never have got to know Damian better.

She'd started going over and sitting on his desk and having these whispered conversations with him. Even though I'd begged her not to, I did wonder if she might have been talking about me, which was quite exciting. But if ever I asked what they'd talked about, Cassie would grin and say, 'That's for me to know and you to find out.' Then she always added, 'Trust me, Izz. I'm only doing it for you.' And I knew that was true. Cassie could be a bit bossy, and tell me who I could be friends with, but she was only looking out for me. Not trying to spoil my fun, like Max!

After that, Damian started to come over at breaktimes to talk to us. I still felt really shy, but Cassie did most of the talking anyway. It was a bit like mealtimes with Chip: if you wanted any food you had to get in quick. Even when Damian tried to ask *me* a question, Cassie always jumped in first, making jokes. I'm sure she was just trying to make things easier for me, but some of the things she said to him!

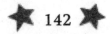

'You're outrageous,' Damian told Cassie one time, smiling at her, and I suddenly wished I could be outrageous, just once, so he'd say that to me. Cassie told me she was sure Damian liked me, but I wasn't so convinced any more. I wasn't funny and *outrageous* like Cassie. But he did still sometimes smile that lovely smile at me.

Cassie had kept on about inviting Damian to Alton Towers, but I never took her seriously, so it came as a shock when I found out that someone else had!

When Auntie Paula told me she needed to book the tickets so I'd better decide exactly who I wanted to take with me, Max was there too. I could feel her watching me.

'I've asked Cassie,' I said straight out. Max just fumed.

'Do you want anyone else as well?' Auntie Paula asked, 'because it is your birthday.' But I shook my head. 'Well, that leaves room for Chip and Max.

Max pulled a disgusted face. 'Please! You can count me out,' she said, as if her mum had suggested taking her to a playschool party.

'Then Chip can take Danny,' Auntie Paula suggested.

Chip looked embarrassed, finally he said, 'I don't think so, Mum. Remember how sick he was the last time? He puked after every ride.'

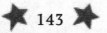

'Thanks Chip, I'd rather not be reminded of that little pleasure,' Auntie Paula said. 'So who will you take?'

He tried to look as if it was no big deal. 'Damian,' he said.

I must have turned to Chip with my mouth open.

'Damian de Blanc?!' Max shrieked with laughter. 'Since when have you been in with that poser?'

For once Chip didn't manage to ignore Max. In fact he looked quite sheepish. His ears turned pink. 'Actually, he's not a poser,' he said. 'He's got what you're always banging on about – style.' Then he got up and left the kitchen.

Max turned her icy stare on me.

'Am I missing something here?' Auntie Paula looked from Max to me. I shrugged. I'd had nothing to do with it, but I couldn't hide the fact that I was pleased.

'Everyone but me is clearly going mad,' Max said, getting up and pushing her chair back. 'Stark staring mad.'

The next day at school, I couldn't wait to tell Cassie, 'You're never going to believe who Chip's taking to Alton Towers.'

'Damian?' she said, looking really smug.

How did she know? I opened my hands and looked completely mystified.

'You know Chip'll do anything – if you pay him enough. It only cost a fiver,' she said. 'But, hey, I got it out my mum's purse anyway. It'll be worth it.'

I didn't know what to say about any of that. Once before, I'd made the mistake of looking shocked when Cassie had talked about stealing from her mum's purse and she'd snapped, 'Oh, please. Don't tell me you've never nicked off your mum, little goody-goody!' I didn't want her thinking I still wasn't cool with it, so this time I just grinned, as if it was no big deal.

'Anyway, Cutie, I thought you'd be pleased,' she said. 'He's not coming to hang out with drippy Chip! So maybe you'd better get some kissing practice in.'

Again I tried not to look as shocked, or as scared, as I felt. I was glad when the bell went for afternoon school, before my face completely gave me away.

By the time I got home, I felt like having a real go at Chip, but then I thought: what's the point. Why had I even been surprised? It was about money after all. And, of course, I did want Damian to come. It was going to be great. If there was still any tiny chance he liked me – and if I could just get over how scared the idea of kissing made me – it would be the most perfect birthday ever.

My only worry was that Mum might suddenly decide she wanted me home before my birthday.

After that I really didn't care, just as long as nothing happened to spoil my day at Alton Towers. Even Max's nagging couldn't burst my bubble. And there was still plenty of that going on.

Because Chip had invited Damian to Alton Towers, he and Danny had had a big fall out, which Max completely blamed on me.

'I hope you're pleased with yourself,' she said. 'Do you know how many years Danny and Chip have been best mates?'

I told Max it wasn't my fault. I hadn't asked Chip to invite Damian. So Max asked me straight out if it had been Cassie's idea. I didn't really want to tell her an outright lie, but I didn't see what it had to do with her anyway. In the end when I wouldn't say yes or no, Max looked as if she'd cracked some kind of mystery.

'Just as I suspected,' she said, like she was Sherlock Holmes or something. '*You* are heading for a bumpy landing any time now, and when it comes you'll only have yourself to blame.'

I just thought that was more of Max's nagging. But a week later, when I *literally* landed with a bump, I felt as if Max must have worked a spell on me – only this time it wasn't a good fairy godmother's makeover spell, it was more like a bad fairy's curse.

twenty-three

'Three detentions in one week, Izzy!' Auntie Paula said, shaking her head. 'I can't believe it. I had no idea things were going so badly for you at school. You seemed to have settled in so well. Is it this new friend Cassie's influence?'

I was sitting at the kitchen table after school, facing Auntie Paula but not daring to look her in the eye. I shook my head. I really wasn't bothered if she blamed me, but I didn't want her blaming Cassie. The only two things I was worried about was whether she'd tell my mum – because I really didn't want Mum to be upset – and, even more importantly, whether I'd lose my birthday trip. But I needn't have worried; Auntie Paula didn't want to go upsetting Mum any more than I did.

'I won't tell your mum this time,' she said. 'But listen, Izzy, if you're upset – or there's anything troubling you – I want you to talk to me. OK?' I nodded and got up to make a quick escape. But Auntie Paula wasn't finished yet. 'Mr Hathaway says he hasn't seen much homework from you lately either. Now would be a good opportunity.'

By the time I'd got my books together, Chip was already sitting at the table in the lounge, surrounded by his.

'Thanks a bundle, Izzy?' he growled. I looked at him surprised. What had I done? 'Because of you, Mum's on my case as well.'

I shrugged and sat down opposite him. It wasn't fair, Chip blaming me. I knew exactly whose fault it was, and just then she walked through the door. Max looked around and grinned, 'Mmm, is this the Referral Room?'

I gave her a really evil look and she rounded on me. 'You don't need to look at me like that. I didn't tell Mum.'

'If you didn't, who did?' I snapped at her.

'School of course, you idiot. They often ring home when you get detentions, especially if there's a lot of them. Didn't you know that?'

'How would I?' I said. 'I'd never had any before I came here.'

'You make it sound as if it's my fault,' Max said. 'I've already had all that from Mum. How could I have known what kind of a monster you'd turn into? If I had I'd never have started on that stupid makeover. I'd have left you like the little mouse you were. At least you were a *nice* mouse! Now I know just how Dr Frankenstein must have felt.'

Max turned her back and left the room. For a minute or two Chip and I looked at each other in

amazement, then suddenly he did this brilliant impression of Frankenstein's monster and we both fell about laughing.

Max's voice came floating downstairs, 'I'm glad you two find it so funny.'

Later when I thought about what she'd said, I couldn't believe how wrong Max'd got it. Before the makeover I was a real nobody. I wasn't even a nice little mouse like she said. I was just a coward, afraid to say what I thought. Now I was getting braver all the time, thanks to Cassie. I was starting to stand up for myself. I wasn't Bella any more, I was Izzy right through. And Max didn't like it because she was jealous, that now I'd got Cassie I didn't need her any more.

But that blow-up with Max was only a hiccup really. That wasn't the bumpy landing. Not yet.

A week before the trip to Alton Towers, Mum found out about my money.

It happened on Friday night when Auntie Paula told Mum about the birthday plan and Mum had a mini-fit – about how the rides weren't safe, how I might fall off – or out of – or under one of them. I could lose a leg, an arm, my life – at the very least an eye! I might get lost, mugged, abducted, never seen again. Blah, blah, blah. That's just how my mum's mind always works.

But after a lot of persuasion Auntie Paula

managed to calm her down and convince her it wasn't the most dangerous place on the planet – that Max and Chip had been a few times and were still alive with all their limbs intact.

By the time Mum spoke to me on the phone she seemed to be coming round to the idea of letting me go. But then she insisted that Auntie Paula had been too good to me already and that I should use my own money to pay for the trip – out of my account!

I panicked and quickly put Auntie Paula back on the phone. She decided that now was the time to tell Mum how little of it was actually left. Oh, big mistake.

My mum went bananas! She went on and on to Auntie Paula and then insisted on speaking to me again. I tried to reason with her but she wouldn't listen.

'Go upstairs and pack your things, *straight away!*' she said. 'I want you home *this weekend.*'

I couldn't bear it. I was angrier than I'd ever been in my whole life and this time I didn't care whether I upset Mum or not. All I cared about right now was my birthday trip. 'I'm not coming home,' I said. 'Not until *after* my birthday. And *you* can't make me.' I couldn't believe it, but I'd said it.

Then Mum started getting upset. 'How do you think that makes me feel,' she said, 'you not wanting to come home? After all I've been

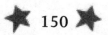

through.' I could hear her starting to cry, but I still didn't care. I just exploded again.

'In case you've forgotten, *you* made me come here. I didn't want to come in the first place. But it never matters what I want. You want me back now, when it suits you. Just like you only talk about what suits you. I'm not a baby any more, and you can't treat me like one.' Then I hung up the phone and burst into tears.

It took Auntie Paula ages to calm me down. She said she'd ring Mum back later, when *she'd* had time to calm down, and talk her round. She said she was sure she'd be able to. But I wasn't holding my breath. They were on the phone for ages and Auntie Paula looked really serious afterwards. But she said that Mum had finally agreed to let me stay and go to Alton Towers, but that they both thought it was probably best I went home soon after my birthday.

It was a couple of days before Mum and me talked again on the phone. When we did Mum sounded as if she was being really careful what she said and so was I. She didn't even mention the money, which suited me.

But all that wasn't the bumpy landing either...

The week of my birthday things got really bad at school. Cassie and me seemed to be getting into more and more trouble with Mr Hathaway. He'd

started calling us the Hyenas, because we were always laughing really loud at some joke or other. And it's true, the more Hayley and her creepy crowd looked down their noses at us, the louder we got.

I suppose it was because of Damian that I really started feeling sort of desperate. I'd only got a few days left to show him that I could be outrageous like Cassie. I wanted to prove to him – and myself – once and for all, that I wasn't boring little Bella the mouse.

On Wednesday, before registration, Cassie and me were sharing a bottle of coke and it made us both burp. So then we got into a sort of burping contest. When Mr Hathaway came in we stopped burping, of course, but then I got the hiccups and we both just lost it. The more I hiccupped, the more Cassie laughed. You know how when you're told by a teacher to *stop laughing or else* it just makes you worse, well, Cassie laughed so much she fell off her chair.

Lots of people in the class were laughing as well by then and I don't know what got into us, but we started chasing each other round the classroom. I didn't care if I got a whole string of detentions, what did it matter now? I was going home, back to my boring old life.

Mr Hathaway kept telling us to calm down, but it was like I couldn't even hear him. It was like I

was inside that goldfish bowl again, in my own world, and everyone else was outside. I knew I was probably screaming with laughter; I think I was a bit hysterical.

Suddenly, I saw Damian watching us and smiling. I thought, this is it; this is my chance to show him. I might not get another one. So I jumped straight onto his desk and Cassie jumped up after me. We started dancing up there with everyone in the class watching us.

Lots of the boys were cheering and clapping, giving us a beat to dance to. Then someone put some music on, I don't know how. But we really went for it then. It felt fantastic – the most exciting and outrageous thing I'd ever done. I wished Max could see me. For the first time since my scary fairy godmother's makeover I really did feel like a wild child – through and through – and I didn't want it to stop.

But of course it did. I got *so* wild that in the end I lost my balance and grabbed hold of Cassie. When I fell off the desk, I pulled her down with me and I landed with my right leg bent underneath me – with Cassie on top of it.

The first thought that went through my head was, *Owww!*

The next one was: you idiot, how can you go to Alton Towers if you've broken your ankle?

twenty-four

Max handed me the tray and went and lay on her bed and watched me eat my supper. I could tell she'd have just loved to be sitting there gloating – *told you so* written all over her face. But Auntie Paula was putting so much of the blame on Max, she couldn't really enjoy the fact that I'd badly sprained my ankle. It made Max even madder that Auntie Paula was being so soft on me. I knew that it was because Auntie Paula thought I'd got into most of the trouble through worrying about my mum being ill – which only made me feel worse because she was wrong, of course. I wasn't Bella, who worried about things, I was wild-child Izzy now, with cool friends like Cassie, and there was no going back. But I couldn't explain that to Auntie Paula.

'I'm sick of Mum blaming me,' Max kept on moaning. 'I've told her I was the one that warned you from the beginning about staying out of trouble. And away from Cassie McCloud!'

Max had been going on like this ever since my accident. I'd had to miss the last two days of

school which meant Auntie Paula had had to take time off work and that was really difficult for her with her job. So as soon as Max came in from school each night, Auntie Paula made *her* run up and downstairs after me instead, which made Max's blood boil.

Apart from Max, though, I was stuck there completely on my own. No one rang from school. I was a bit disappointed that Cassie hadn't. I texted her:

R U OK? DID U HURT URSELF?

And she texted me back:

BRUISED BUM THAT'S ALL.

But then I didn't hear from her again. I guessed she was worried she'd get the blame if she called at the house.

I felt sick every time I thought about what an idiot I'd made of myself – and in front of Damian. And I could just imagine how delighted Hayley and the others were that I'd finally…well, fallen off my perch.

When Mum rang we had to play down how badly swollen my ankle was or she'd have had me home in a second. Now I had just two days left before my birthday trip on Sunday to get back on my feet. Auntie Paula told me that if I stayed where I was, with my ankle up, and we kept giving it the ice and heat treatment, I should still be able to go to Alton Towers.

What was worrying me was that if the swelling didn't go down I wouldn't get my boots on, but Auntie Paula just shook her head and smiled slightly. 'I'd have thought those boots were the least of your worries,' she told me.

As soon as I could put some weight on my ankle, Auntie Paula insisted that Max help me to exercise my ankle. We were still hardly speaking, but I had to let her help me to limp round the bedroom.

'I don't understand why you aren't racing to go home, now this has happened,' Max grumbled at me. 'I know I would be. Aren't you missing your mum? I don't understand why this trip to Alton Towers is such a mega-big deal.'

Of course I was missing Mum, but more than anything, I wanted to have this birthday trip – this one last adventure – before I had to go back to being boring Bella again. I wanted something exciting to take home with me. Max didn't understand, it wasn't about Alton Towers, it was about having real fun, like Max probably had every birthday of her life. Mum had never let me have a proper big birthday party, with lots of friends. We usually did something quiet, just the two of us, or Dawn came to tea if I was lucky. Even if by some miracle Mum did decide to take me somewhere exciting, and let Dawn come with me (if she was still talking to me, of course), Mum would be bound to

spoil it by following us round, fussing and worrying. Whereas Chip had told me that at Alton Towers Auntie Paula usually found the nearest coffee shop and left them to it most of the day.

But I didn't try to explain any of that to Max. How could she ever begin to understand? I looked her straight in the eye instead and said, 'I just want to have some fun, OK?! Do you remember *fun*? You're the one who told me that's what it's all about – before you turned into a nag. You're just like my mum – you can't bear for me to have a good time. Well, on Sunday I'm going to have the best, wildest birthday ever with Damian and Cassie – she *does* know how to have fun. And thank goodness, neither you nor my mum will be there to spoil it.'

I was quite surprised Max actually looked hurt. But at least, for once, she looked as if she was really thinking about what I'd said. 'OK,' she replied at last, 'I get it. You want it to be a really special birthday. You want it to be perfect.' And I thought, maybe she sort of understood. Fat chance. If I had only known *what* she was thinking – what scheme was going through her head right then – I would have been *so* angry, my scary fairy godmother would have been scared of *me*.

When I hadn't heard from Cassie by Friday morning I started worrying whether she was still

coming to Alton Towers. In the end I had to ask Chip to find out. Chip had told me that Damian had gone a bit cool on the idea at first, which wasn't surprising after the idiot I'd made of myself on his desk. But when he came home on Friday Chip said they were both definitely coming: Cassie had managed to persuade Damian. I wondered how she'd done that – and whether she'd said anything to him about me.

And then on Saturday morning, for no obvious reason, Max decided that *she* was coming too. Chip complained it was going to be a squeeze in the back seat of the car, but as usual Max got her own way.

Right from the start I should have spotted the clues on my birthday morning. They were all there. Max was being far too nice to me. She couldn't seem to get me out of bed fast enough, and help me downstairs. And then she wouldn't let me move out of the chair.

'There'll be lots of walking at Alton Towers,' she kept reminding me. 'You've got to rest that ankle.'

Another clue was the whispered chat she had with Mum when she rang to wish me Happy Birthday. The smarmy smile on her face when she handed the phone over to me. And the knowing smiles between her and Auntie Paula.

And then, when I kept remembering things I

wanted from the bedroom, she offered to run upstairs to fetch them, or sent Chip, rather than letting me go back up there. When we got into the car, Max insisted I sit in the front seat, so I'd have room to stretch my leg out, which meant she'd have to sit in the back – with Cassie – and even then she didn't complain! Oh, I definitely should have smelled a rat! It would have been called Maxine.

There was also some funny business about all the stuff that was being packed in the back of the car. The boot opened and closed with a bang five or six times. I thought it was probably the picnic and my birthday cake – Auntie Paula had asked me a week ago what my favourite kind was – chocolate, obviously – so I didn't say anything. I didn't want to spoil the surprise. How dumb was I!

When Damian and Cassie arrived that was a surprise too, because they arrived together. Cassie said her dad's car was off the road. She was wearing a great outfit: a wide necked top that showed her shoulders, a pair of jeans folded over in deep cuffs and big hoop earrings and a pair of shoes with heels. She looked as cool as Max and I hoped Max would notice!

'You look fantastic,' I told her.

She smiled and said, 'Oh, thanks.' Then she fiddled with my hair a bit where I'd tried to do it like hers and hadn't got it exactly right. She

didn't ask me how my ankle was.

When Max finally got into the car, she was red in the face, as if she'd run up and down stairs twenty times or more. She nodded at Damian but she didn't even look at Cassie. I wished Max wasn't coming. I just hoped that when we got to Alton Towers she'd keep her mum company and with a bit of luck, Cassie and Damian and Chip and me could go off and do anything we wanted. This was going to be the most exciting birthday ever and even with a bad ankle, I was determined nothing was going to spoil it.

I was a bit disappointed I couldn't be in the back seat, having fun with the others. They were all squeezed up so tight that Cassie was nearly on Damian's knee. I tried to catch Cassie's eye a few times but she was too busy laughing and talking about the different rides. Chip was telling them which were the best ones – which ones were the scariest.

It was the first time I'd stopped and thought, oh my goodness, what if I'm too scared to go on any of them? What if when I get there I turn back into boring Bella – too scared to go on anything apart from the little kids' rides? I really couldn't bear the thought of embarrassing myself in front of Damian and Cassie. Suddenly, I was glad I was in the front and no one could see me squirming in my seat.

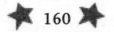 160

*

I had no idea that Alton Towers was going to be such a massive place. After we parked we had to take a monorail to get to the main entrance. It was a really bright morning and the sun was shining on the lake. The whole place seemed completely magic and I thought: this is how the whole day's going to be.

I was almost jumping up and down with excitement and nerves, trying to take it all in. Chip was ready to get going and started to head off towards the rides, until Auntie Paula called him back.

'Hang on a minute,' she said. 'What's the hurry? Before you all go wandering off, let's have a plan, shall we?'

'Synchronise watches,' Chip said, checking his with Auntie Paula's.

'We'll meet back here for lunch at two o'clock,' she said.

And then we were all desperate to get off on our own – to have the next three hours to completely please ourselves. I'd noticed Max out of the corner of my eye, looking very odd, glancing around as if she was expecting to see someone. And sharing looks with Auntie Paula.

Suddenly her face broke into this huge grin and she started waving.

I turned to see who it could be. And there

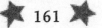

was…*my mum*, in that revolting red wig – walking towards us.

I stood there, sort of paralysed, thinking: oh no, not now, Mum, not here, not today. I know it's horrible, but I couldn't help it – I just wanted to run away and pretend I didn't even know her.

twenty-five

'Hello, sweetheart,' Mum called. 'Surprise!'

My mouth fell wide open, like a cartoon character's, landing thud on the floor. And then my mum grabbed me in this big hug, so I could hardly breathe. Over her shoulder I could see Max – looking like someone who'd done something really clever and couldn't wait for everyone else to hear about it.

'Max thought it would be an extra birthday surprise,' Auntie Paula explained, smiling as if she was so proud of her. 'It was all her idea.'

I thought, I'll bet it was. So this was the evil scheme that had been going through my mean and bossy fairy godmother's head. She knew that having my mum here would spoil the whole day's fun for me. I knew that was why she'd set this up – on purpose to get at me. And that wasn't all of it.

Max and Mum hugged too, like they were old pals suddenly. Then she did a half-whisper thing, like they do in pantomimes, when really everyone's meant to hear: 'It's all organised. Her bags are in the boot. She didn't suspect a thing.'

She was clearly me. And Max was right, I didn't. I hadn't guessed that Max was so desperate and determined to get rid of me that she'd packed up everything I owned and hidden it in the boot of Auntie Paula's car.

'Coming home at last! Won't that be lovely?' Mum asked, hugging me even tighter. 'Happy Birthday, Bella, sweetheart.'

I can't remember ever feeling so angry. Not even when I was five and the boy next door broke my brand new bike and I bit him. I suddenly remembered exactly how it had felt, and how my mum had been so ashamed of me that she'd hardly spoken to me for two days afterwards.

Now, even though I was almost choking with anger – and once again felt like biting someone – I had to completely cover it up. How could I get angry with my mum standing there, her eyes all full up with tears because she was so pleased to see me. My mum who'd been so ill, who was holding onto my hand so tightly as if I might disappear if she let it go.

I tried to smile back at her, even though I could see Cassie and Damian grinning at me. I think I managed to say, 'It's great, Mum.' But mostly I just concentrated on keeping my eyes – *and my hands* – off Max's grinning face. I thought of that conversation we'd had, right back at the beginning, when Max had said she didn't

believe that I never got really mad. Well, I was really, *really* mad now and it was all down to her.

My mum was still hugging me. I could see Cassie looking at Damian in embarrassment and I wanted to crawl into a hole, even before Mum started having a go at me. I don't think she meant anyone else to hear, but everyone did.

'Oh, *no!*' she groaned. 'Please don't tell me you've had your ears pierced! Oh, Bella. Oh, no.'

Auntie Paula tried to rescue me. 'They've all got them now, Lynda. It's nothing.'

But Mum shook her head. 'I can't believe it. Look at you, I can't believe how much you've changed.'

'Please, Mum,' I tried to get her to stop, but she just kept on...

'You'd never have chosen to come *here* before, either. You've always been terrified of these places. Do you remember when you screamed so much I had to take you off the merry-go-round?'

'I was *three!*' I almost shouted at her.

Everyone else was laughing now and I think Mum realised for a minute how much she was embarrassing me. She tried to give me another cuddle. I just wanted to run away and leave Mum standing there. The last thing I wanted was for the others to go off, leaving me on my own with her. But that was Max's next bright idea.

'Come on, Mum,' she said. 'I think Izzy wants

some time with her mum.'

Auntie Paula looked a bit unsure, but Max went on pulling at her sleeve and the others were only too pleased to make their getaway. I watched them all go, Cassie and Damian walking with their heads together, laughing. I would never forgive Max for this. Or my mum.

All I could think was: why did she have to come and spoil my dream day? Why was she already trying to turn me back into Bella, in front of everybody? I couldn't bear it.

I felt like I might explode. And then, when Mum wouldn't stop hugging me, I did.

'What are you *doing* here, Mum?!' I yelled.

She looked really surprised and pulled back as if I'd hit her.

'I thought you'd be pleased to see me on your birthday.'

'Pleased?!' I practically screamed. 'You come here, embarrassing me in front of my friends…making sure I don't have any fun, just like you always do.'

'What on earth do you mean?' Mum demanded.

'You've never liked me having friends,' I insisted.

'That's nonsense.'

'It's why I'm such a sad and boring person, always worrying about *nothing* – just like you.'

My mum's eyes started to fill with tears. 'Oh,

Bella, I didn't mean to...' but I didn't let her finish, it was all still pouring out of me and I couldn't stop it.

'Don't *call* me that!' I really screamed at her this time.

'But it's your name.'

'It's not. Not any more. You already said: *Bella* isn't the kind of person who'd want to come to a place like Alton Towers.'

'Yes, well I agree with Bella,' Mum started again. 'Most of these rides look like death traps to me.'

'It's called *fun*, Mum,' I snapped at her, remembering what Max had once said to me. 'You've heard of *fun*, right?'

'Oh, sweetheart, of course I have,' Mum said, trying to take hold of my hand. 'Look, I know this has been a miserable time and I can see a lot of things have changed Bella, and—'

But I didn't want to stay there another minute listening to my mum going on about how I'd changed, *as if it was a bad thing*. As if boring Bella was someone you'd choose to be, not avoid at all costs! I wanted to be off, catching up with the others before I lost them completely.

I know it sounds mean, but suddenly I couldn't stop myself pushing her away, and racing off as fast as my bad ankle would let me.

I hurried past Auntie Paula and Max – they were sitting on a bench just round the corner. I

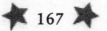

didn't even look at them but I could feel their eyes on me.

By the time I caught up with the others I knew they'd been talking about me. Cassie said, 'Oh, *Bella!*' and rolled her eyes at Damian. Then she leaned towards me, grinning. 'Is that a wig your mum's wearing?'

For a minute I wanted to yell at her, *Yes, because she's got cancer and all her hair's fallen out, OK!!* And that's what I should have done. But I didn't, of course. I couldn't bear to fall out with my super-cool friend, Cassie, because I still wanted us to have the best day ever. And for that I was determined to be Izzy, so I laughed instead.

'Yeah, gross, isn't it?'

Once we got to the rides the others got so excited they kept forgetting about my ankle and leaving me behind. But however much it hurt I was determined I was going to keep up with them.

Chip said we should check out *Oblivion* first. He and Damian were arguing whether *Oblivion* was more awesome than *Nemesis*. But to me everything looked awesome: the size of the rides, the speed of them, the sound of people screaming as we went past. It all made my head spin.

When we came to *Oblivion* the noise became even more deafening because the track ran right over our heads. I'd seen roller-coasters before,

small ones, but nothing like this.

The cars were wide enough to hold about sixteen people. They travelled along a track which rose right up in the air and then suddenly the track just dropped away, and so did the cars – like they'd reached the edge of a cliff and thrown themselves off. I couldn't understand why they didn't just fly off the track, or fire everyone out like a catapult.

To make it even more scary – if that was possible – when the car got to the edge, just before it fell, it stopped and hung there in mid-air, for about a minute, to let you see how far you were going to fall. Then, when it dropped, it was so fast, people's faces rushed past in a blur, their arms flung out in terror, before they disappeared into a great, big black hole in the ground.

It was wild! Just watching it made my heart race and I had to hold onto a railing because I felt dizzy. But when Cassie said, 'Bit too scary for you, eh, *Bella*?' I was determined not to let her see I was terrified. Especially not with Damian there as well.

I was glad when Chip suggested we left *Oblivion* till the queues went down. He said we could go on some of the tamer rides first, although I hadn't seen anything I'd have called tame yet.

When we came to one called *Enterprise*, Chip said we should start with that. It was a huge wheel on the ground with individual cars fixed to

it. The cars were really meant for one person, but some older boys and their girlfriends were getting in together and squeezing up tight. Damian got into the first one and, without saying a word to me, Cassie quickly pushed past and got into it with him. Then she looked back and gave me this silly grin. I was so surprised I didn't know what to do, but when the next car came along, Chip nudged me and I quickly got into it. He got into the next one.

The man locked us in and the ride started. I was still so mad with Max, and my mum, and confused about Cassie getting into the car with Damian, that I didn't start to feel nervous again until the cars had already begun to speed up. Soon they were swinging right out at the side and going faster and faster and then the whole wheel rose up on its side until we were going *even* faster, flying way, way up in the air.

I couldn't help it, I found myself screaming. And then it felt as if I was full of screams that had been waiting to get out for years. Other people around me were screaming too, but no one as loud as me. It felt…*fantastic*!

You see, Bella, I told myself, look what you've been missing!

twenty-six

Luckily, before I could lose my nerve again, we went straight on another ride called *Spinball Whizzer*. This time, the cars held about eight people and ran on a huge rollercoaster track, but whizzed round at the same time really fast like a waltzer.

When the car arrived in front of us, Damian got in first and then, just as Chip went to follow him, Cassie pushed past again. 'Ladies first,' she said, grinning, which left me at the end of the row.

It was pretty slow to begin with and, like an idiot, I thought it wasn't going to be too bad. But eventually it went so fast, I thought I was going to *die!* Every time it changed direction we were thrown against each other and Chip and I nearly banged heads. Cassie was hanging onto Damian as if she was really scared. I was *terrified* but I wouldn't have dared grab hold of a boy – even Chip – and he's my cousin. But once I started to scream again I really got into it and then I didn't want it to stop. Ever!

When it finally did and we had to get off and

everyone was saying it was good – but a bit tame – I didn't mention I'd been scared at first. I just joined in and agreed with them. I told myself, this is how I'd hoped it would be. It was so cool. I could probably have done with a minute or two to get my breath back and rest my ankle, which was hurting… but everyone was off again.

'Come on, Slowcoach, keep up,' Chip shouted.

And then Cassie started calling me Hop-a-Long.

Even though the three of them were together out in front, with me trailing behind, I told myself it didn't matter, I was still one of the gang. Damian looked back once or twice and I hoped he'd give me one of those smiles like he sometimes used to at school. But he just turned back to Cassie and no one waited for me to catch up.

Ahead of us was the castle with a lake in front. It's a real castle that the theme park's built around. Most of it's falling down, but in one part there's something called *Hex* which is a sort of spooky, Haunted Castle kind of ride.

'Let's go in here,' Cassie squealed.

I usually hate spooky things, at least Bella always has, but the others were heading straight over there so I reminded myself that I was Izzy, gave myself a shake, and followed them. But by the time I got to the entrance, they'd all disappeared. I hurried inside, into the first room which was quite gloomy, and peered around to

see if I could see them, but it was too dark to see anyone properly.

Everyone was looking up at TV screens that told you this ghost story with ghostly music in the background. There were weird statues along the walls. It was all pretty creepy and I didn't want to go any further, but everyone was pushing forwards into the next room, and I just got carried along with them.

I felt completely miserable. I was lost in the middle of a huge crowd of strangers, worried I wouldn't find the others. I wasn't even sure Cassie wanted me to find them. What was going on? Why was she flirting with Damian? She'd told me *she* didn't fancy him. Well, it wasn't looking like that. If she was 'only doing it for me', like she'd told me before, it didn't make any sense.

I was desperate to get out of that horrible place. I didn't think I could hang on to being Izzy much longer. Then, just when the panic was about to take over, the crowd surged forward and we headed towards the light and the exit. Once I was outside I just followed the crowd, half-limping as fast as I could, hoping to catch up with the others.

Just as I came round a corner of the castle, way ahead of me, I saw Cassie's gold earrings flash in the sun and Damian's white sweatshirt and jeans, though no sign of Chip. I called out for them to

wait for me, but they were already running far ahead, down a path in the opposite direction. And then I noticed – they were holding hands! Even an idiot like me couldn't mistake that, and now I could see what was going on. I stopped racing and suddenly noticed how much my ankle was hurting.

'You're *so* dumb, Izzy,' I told myself. 'As dumb as Bella.'

And just then, when I was feeling completely miserable, guess who popped up by my side to rub it in.

'Found you at last,' Max gasped. 'I've been looking everywhere for you. Where have Chip and the others gone?'

'I don't know – I couldn't keep up. I've got a bad ankle, haven't I?' I snapped, in case she'd forgotten.

'Your mum's really upset, you know. You just ran off. We were all worried you wouldn't know your way around.'

I couldn't believe how badly things had turned out, in every possible way, and suddenly I was yelling, 'Don't start. Having my mum here's bad enough, without you joining in. Yeah! You invited her to spite me, didn't you?'

'Of course, I didn't…' Max started.

But I knew what she was up to. 'You brought Mum here because you knew it would ruin my

day. You knew she'd fuss and complain and make sure I didn't get on any rides. That she'd embarrass me in front of everyone by treating me like a baby!'

'Look, it wasn't like that…' Max tried again.

'I'm sick of her and I'm sick of you – always telling me what to do. I wish I'd never come to your horrible house!' I hissed in Max's face, then I turned and headed back the way we'd first come, hoping Max would finally leave me alone. But I should have known that was never going to happen. She caught up with me easily as I limped along.

'I thought you'd *want* to see your mum,' she tried to explain. 'I did it for your own good, Izzy. And to get you away from Cassie McCloud, before she got you into any more trouble.'

Just hearing Cassie's name again made me sink even lower. I knew how pleased Max would be to find she'd been right about her, to be able to say *I told you so*. But I still couldn't help blurting it out, 'Why did she do it? I told her how much I liked Damian?'

Max just shrugged. 'To prove she can. Probably.'

I remembered then that was exactly what Hayley had said. What a stupid, stupid idiot I'd been. They'd all tried to warn me, especially Max, but I'd thought they were being bitchy or jealous. I hadn't believed them because I'd wanted to

think that someone as cool as Cassie would want to hang out with me. But Hayley was probably right; Cassie had only gone after me because Hayley wanted me, like she'd decided to go after Damian for herself, just because she knew I wanted him. And I hadn't seen any of that, because I'd been too busy pretending to be Izzy, cool and couldn't care less. And look where that had got me.

Without realising it, I'd been heading back towards *Oblivion*. Suddenly there was so much screaming overhead I could hardly hear what Max was saying to me. It was such a relief. I couldn't bear the way the day had gone so wrong. I'd been desperate to hang onto a little bit of Izzy, just for this one last day, before Mum took me home and I finally turned back into boring Bella. But there wasn't much chance of that left. I was starting to feel as if I'd never been Izzy in the first place – not really. I'd failed at that too.

I certainly didn't want to hear any more of Max's explanations and when she tried to persuade me to go back and find Mum and Auntie Paula – because they were so worried about me – I was ready to do almost anything to get away from her.

And I heard myself saying, 'Sorry, Max, it'll have to wait. I'm going on *Oblivion*. See ya.'

twenty-seven

That's how I found myself in the queue for the scariest ride at Alton Towers. At least, I told myself, I'd finally shaken off my evil, bossy fairy godmother. She was probably sucking up to my mum right at that moment. But getting rid of Max was never going to be that easy. Minutes later she came pushing along the queue to reach me, still going on at me.

'I did it because I was trying to make your birthday even more perfect, Izzy.'

She could tell by my face that I didn't believe that.

'And because I was worried about you.'

'Worried about me?!' I snapped at her.

'About what you'd turned into. I wanted to get you home, to your mum, back to your old self, the sooner the better, away from *bad influences*. You need your mum and she needs you. I know I started it all off with that stupid makeover, but it's gone to your head. You've turned into a real brat.'

'Oh, you think so, do you?' I yelled at Max. 'What if I'd rather be a brat? What if I don't

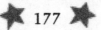

want to go back to being myself: boring! wimpy! pathetic!'

'You weren't like that. At least you cared about other people's feelings before. Now you're just a clone of Cassie McCloud. That's not being yourself! It's being a mug and remember; mugs aren't cool.'

'Neither are nags!' I shouted back at her.

Soon we were doing so much shouting a few people queuing round us were staring, but it didn't stop us.

'If I was so OK, why did you have to interfere?' I asked her.

'It was just a game. It wasn't supposed to be for real. I just meant to liven you up a bit, not turn you into a monster!'

'You're the monster,' I yelled. 'Trying to take over someone else's life.'

'I was trying to help!' Max screamed at me.

'I never asked for your help,' I screamed back. 'I wouldn't want it if we were locked in the same room together for the rest of our lives!'

Now everyone was staring at us. I hadn't even realised we'd reached the end of the queue and an empty car was waiting in front of us. I was too angry to even think about it. The man said, 'Hurry up. Move along. Move right along the seat.'

Max followed me into the car, but she left a gap you could have fitted an elephant in. Soon other

people were piling in after us and in the end she had to slide right up next to me. Then it was just Max – my evil, bossy, scary fairy godmother – and me, heading into *Oblivion*.

With every second that went by I felt I was turning back into Bella. My mouth was completely dry and my legs were shaking. But I couldn't let Max see that. I suddenly wished I'd gone to the loo first. What if I got so scared I wet myself? Max would never let me forget it.

At first we rolled slowly along the track. I'd gone really cold. I tried to remind myself that I'd managed the other rides: *Enterprise* and *Spinball Whizzer*, I'd manage *Oblivion*. But I'd stood and watched this ride – I knew it was in a different league. Perhaps if I closed my eyes, I thought, I could pretend it wasn't happening. I tried it, and for a minute or two, I felt almost safe again.

But then I noticed we weren't even moving and I opened my eyes. It was incredible.

We were really high up now and you could see for miles and miles, nothing but blue sky and clouds and the very tops of trees and hills way off in the distance. It was *beautiful*, until I realised we were hanging right over the edge of the rails.

My stomach rose up into my throat. Any second now, I knew we were going to be racing down the tracks – the ground rushing up to swallow us.

But it didn't happen. Instead a recorded

message came loud and clear:

'Oblivion is experiencing a temporary delay.
We are unsure of the length of this delay.
Thank you for being patient.'

People behind us started laughing, making jokes about us being stuck there all day. I didn't know how they could be laughing, I was too scared to even scream.

I tried not to, but I couldn't help looking down. Among the tiny figures on the ground, I recognised a flash of red. It was my mum, in that ridiculous wig. And I could see Auntie Paula. And Chip was with them. Cassie and Damian had obviously given him the slip too.

I could tell from the way Mum kept looking around she was still trying to find me. Still *worrying* about me. My anger flared again for a second. But then something horrible happened. The wind suddenly got up and I saw my mum's stupid wig blow off her head. My mum's hands flew up in the air trying to catch it. But the wig rolled along the ground, leaving her all naked and helpless-looking. Auntie Paula and Chip ran after it, while my mum tried to cover her head with her hands. Then someone started pointing and…laughing, and I realised with horror it was Cassie! A little way off, she and Damian were doubled up with laughter. I felt sick and completely ashamed. I wanted to get off the ride,

 180

rush over and put my arms round her. My poor mum – after all she'd been through.

Only an hour ago *I'd* been laughing at Mum's wig, just like them. I thought, I'm as evil as Cassie! Of course my mum was a worrier and a fuss-pot, but…it was only because she loved me. Bella had always known that, it was Izzy who forgot.

I didn't want to turn and face Max. I was scared she'd see right through me again. I knew Max would *never* have laughed at my mum. If I'd listened to her and been more myself, instead of trying so hard to be cool, I wouldn't have either. Max had cared about my mum and what she was going through, and I owed her an apology.

But when I finally got up the courage to face Max, I saw her face was a horrible grey colour, like cold porridge, and her eyes looked red and watery as if…as if she was struggling not to cry.

When she saw me looking at her she whispered, 'I can't do it, I can't do it.' And suddenly she was trying to unfasten the harness that was holding her in and yelling, 'I've got to get out. I'm gonna be sick, Izzy. I know I'm gonna be sick.'

Of course she couldn't get out. We were all locked in, but that didn't stop her trying. The boy next to her said, 'Take it easy, girl. This happens all the time.' But Max kept on struggling and everyone was looking at her now.

A man in the seat behind put his hand on her

shoulder and told her to just *calm down*. Max told him to go to hell.

'Charming,' he said to me. 'You'd better tell your sister to get a grip, we could be waiting a while yet.' I didn't bother telling him we weren't sisters – that we weren't even friends.

Max's head was shaking from side to side and she kept on saying, 'I can't do this. Oh, help, Izzy. I can't do it.' And then she was crying, real tears running down her face leaving big streaks in her make-up.

I didn't know what to do, I was terrified too, but I told her, 'It's OK, Max. You'll be fine. You can do it.'

Max turned to me with this hopeful look on her face, as if I might have some magic words for *her* for once. 'How?' she said. 'Tell me how, Izzy.' And it felt good for a change to have my cool cousin Max, who seemed to know everything and always had the ideas, asking me for my help and advice.

I squeezed her hand and smiled at her. 'You'll be OK,' I said. 'Don't be scared, Max. We'll get through it together.'

twenty-eight

They kept repeating the message every few minutes, thanking us for being patient. I couldn't wait for them to fix the problem, even though I knew we'd still have that stomach-churning drop to come. When you're as high up as that, one way or another you've got to come down.

I realised that my life ever since I'd been living with Max had been just like *Oblivion*: I'd been right up in the air; I'd felt like I was flying. Everything had been new and different, exciting – and scary at times. But now I was ready to come down to earth. I wanted to go home – to my mum. To be with someone that I didn't always have to pretend with.

Ever since I'd been little it felt as if I'd always been scared. Even as Izzy I'd been scared...that people might find out I was scared. I thought you couldn't be scared and cool at the same time. But when I looked at Max, my mega-cool cousin, I could see that even she was scared. It hadn't stopped her following me onto the ride, though, trying to talk some sense

into me. Maybe, if I'd listened to her a bit more, we could have been friends all this time!

Lately, the thing I'd been most scared of had been going home – and turning back into boring old Bella. But now I could see that there were lots of things about Bella that were worth keeping – the nicer bits, the sensible bits. But I wanted to hang on to some bits of Izzy, as well – the braver, more fun bits. And why not? Surely, if I could hold on to my cool, scary cousin – who was trembling like a jelly while we hung over the edge of a cliff – without freaking out myself, I could go home and hold on to a little bit of Izzy?

Suddenly, we heard the sound of machinery starting up. Max squeezed my hand so tight I lost all feeling in it. A split second later the car gave a sickening lurch forward, and it happened – we dropped off the end of the world.

Whooosh!

I'd planned to keep my eyes open the whole way down. I wanted to see everything as it flew past me. But my eyes had other ideas. By the time I realised and opened them again, it was all over. We were under the ground – hurtling through the dark and suddenly the light came rushing to meet us.

We'd both survived and we ended up giggling

like a pair of idiots. Max was still squeezing me tight.

'You can let go of my hand now,' I told her.

'Oh, yeah, thanks,' she said, grinning

It was over so fast, I felt as if I'd missed something. You'll probably think I'm just saying this, but it's the truth: I wanted to get straight back on and do it all over again. I didn't think it would be such a great idea to suggest that to Max, though.

We both agreed it was time to head back. I wanted to see my mum now. I wanted to make sure she was OK.

Max still seemed to think she needed to explain things to me, but I said, 'Look, Max, let's forget it, *please*? It's OK.' But you'd think I'd have known by now who'd have the last word.

'I just want to admit that I went a bit OTT with that makeover. You were OK as you were, you know. More than OK. You just needed a bit of a...brush up.'

'Maybe a bit more than a brush up,' I said. 'I was a total mouse. And,' I admitted, 'I've been terrified I'll turn back into one.'

Max burst out laughing. 'Have you looked at yourself recently. There's no way that's gonna happen. You were fearless up there. Anyway, it is time you went home. You're already too big for those boots. Or should I say, glass slippers?' she added, grinning.

 185

I expected my mum to be in a bit of a strop, but I could tell by her face she was more worried than cross. I went straight over to her when we found them all, and before she could say anything, gave her a big hug. I didn't care what Cassie McCloud might think. Or Damian.

I whispered in Mum's ear, 'I'm *really* sorry. I didn't mean any of it. I've just been so worried about you, about everything.'

Mum smiled and hugged me back.

No one else took any notice of us because Auntie Paula was going on at Max: 'You're practically green, Maxine. Are you OK? What have you been doing?'

I could hear Cassie and Damian talking behind me: 'I think that ride on *Oblivion* was too much for her. She should stick to little kids' rides, like *Bella*.'

I turned and gave them such an evil look.

'We saw you both coming off,' Cassie smirked at me. 'Was it fun?'

'*Oblivion*? Max? Never,' Chip scoffed. 'Not in a month of Sundays.'

'That'll be why she looked like she was about to puke,' Cassie sniggered. 'Not so cool, now. What a wimp.'

And that was it. I didn't stop to think. I turned round and walked straight into Cassie and kept

walking, forcing her backwards away from the others. I didn't want them to hear what I had to say. Damian trailed after us.

'You are worse than a wimp,' I told Cassie, through gritted teeth. 'You're a nasty, stupid troublemaker. Max is worth ten of you. I saw you laughing at my mum. Well, she's got *cancer*, that's why she's got a wig. How does that make you feel, Cassie? Not so cool now, eh?'

Cassie's mouth opened and closed, but she couldn't find anything clever to say for once.

'Don't you dare say another word about anyone in my family,' I said and I snatched the earrings she'd given me out of my ears and threw them at her. 'Next time I want to look cool, I won't choose someone like you to copy.' Then I walked back towards the others.

I really hadn't meant anyone else to hear, but Max must have heard something because she gave me a big smile. Then Auntie Paula went over and told Cassie and Damion they'd better take a walk and come back when they'd found their manners. She said she'd meet them at the car in half an hour and they'd better not be late. I was glad we wouldn't have to say our goodbyes in front of them.

Mum came and put her arm around me. 'Do you mind if we get off now, sweetheart?' she asked. She was looking tired.

'I'm more than ready for home,' I told her and we all headed back to the car park.

When we'd brought the cars together, and we were moving my case out of Auntie Paula's boot, she suddenly shrieked, 'We forgot the birthday cake!'

So we all stood round with lumps of cake in our hands while everyone sang *Happy Birthday* to me.

Auntie Paula was nearly in tears when she said goodbye. 'But it won't be long before we see you two again,' she said, sniffing a bit. 'I'll be up in a couple of weekends' time, so I don't know why I'm crying.' And she started smiling again.

'I might come too,' Max said grinning at me.

I looked over at Mum and she looked ready to cry too. I went and put my arm through hers. 'Of course we'll see them soon,' Mum whispered to me. 'They're family aren't they? And friends, and we all need those.'

Yeah, I thought, they're *real* friends.

Finally, Max and Chip and me stood there a bit awkwardly, trying to decide whether to hug each other. In the end Max and me high-fived and Chip just messed up my hair. Again.

'You'd better promise not to do that next time I see you,' I warned him.

'What's it worth?' he said, grinning. I thought, typical!

We got in the car and I wound the window

down and everyone was calling, 'Bye. Safe journey. Bye, Izzy. Bye.'

As Mum drove towards the exit she sighed, 'Oh, Bella, I'm exhausted and I didn't even go on any rides. Anyway, how's your ankle held out? Aren't you hot in those boots?'

'No,' I said. 'I love them, Mum. They're my very best thing.'

Mum shook her head. 'Well, Paula's been telling me how behind the times I am. In fact, she's given me lots of talking to's lately. I can see there's going to be a few changes to get used to.'

'Yeah,' I agreed. 'I'm not a baby any more, Mum.'

'I know that now,' Mum laughed. 'You're looking very grown up these days,' but this time she made it sound as if that was OK.

'I've changed too, you know,' she said. 'When I got ill, I realised the two of us just weren't enough – for either of us. I should have seen that before. I'm sorry.'

'We'll manage now, though, Mum,' I said. 'Now you're getting better. Won't we?'

Mum reached over and squeezed my hand. We drove for a while without talking. Then she said, 'I didn't *mean* to embarrass you back there.'

But I knew that already. 'I know,' I cut her off.

'And what you said before, about never telling you things. I realise what that was about now...'

There was a catch in Mum's voice but she carried on. 'I've got a photograph – it's the only one I kept – but I can show you if you want. When we get home.' I couldn't seem to speak then; I just ended up nodding. 'Anyway,' Mum said, to fill the silence, 'have you had a good time?'

'By the end…it was the best birthday ever,' I said.

'Well, that's good. And it isn't over yet,' she told me. 'There's a couple more surprises when we get home. I've been doing a bit of decorating.' I looked at her amazed. 'Well, some friends of mine did most of it. Not your room, yet. I thought you'd want to do that yourself. Now you're so grown up!'

I grinned and leaned over a little and rested my head on Mum's arm.

'You know what I'd really like from now on, Mum? If everyone called me *Izzy*. I think Bella makes me sound a bit like a dog.'

Mum almost laughed, but she just stopped herself. 'OK, if that's what you want,' she said a bit doubtfully. 'But what about my lovely Bella?'

'Oh, don't worry,' I told her, 'you haven't seen the last of her.'

'Well, that's OK, then,' said Mum, cheering up. 'Izzy it is, from now on.'

'Cool,' I whispered. Then I leaned back and just watched the miles roll by.

Orchard Red Apples

The Truth Cookie	Fiona Dunbar	1 84362 549 0
Utterly Me, Clarice Bean	Lauren Child	1 84362 304 8
Clarice Bean Spells Trouble	Lauren Child	1 84362 858 9
The Fire Within	Chris d'Lacey	1 84121 533 3
IceFire	Chris d'Lacey	1 84362 373 0
You're Amazing Mr Jupiter	Sue Limb	1 84362 614 4

The Light Witch Trilogy:

Shadowmaster	Andrew Masters	1 84362 187 8
The Time of the Stars	Andrew Masters	1 84362 189 4
The Darkening	Andrew Masters	1 84362 188 6

Do Not Read This Book	Pat Moon	1 84121 435 3
Do Not Read Any Further	Pat Moon	1 84121 456 6
Tower-block Pony	Alison Prince	1 84362 648 9

All priced at £4.99

Orchard Red Apples are available from all good bookshops, or can be ordered direct
from the publisher: Orchard Books, PO BOX 29, Douglas IM99 1BQ
Credit card orders please telephone 01624 836000
or fax 01624 837033 or visit our Internet site: www.wattspub.co.uk
or e-mail: bookshop@enterprise.net for details.

To order please quote title, author and ISBN
and your full name and address.
Cheques and postal orders should be made payable to 'Bookpost plc.'
Postage and packing is FREE within the UK
(overseas customers should add £1.00 per book).

Prices and availability are subject to change.